# You're My Rock

## Brothers From Money 4

A complete and sexy BWWM romance by Shanade White of BWWM Club.

Just before billionaire Nate's mom passes away, she drops a bombshell on him - the man who raised him isn't actually his father!

So Nate takes off to Colorado to find the family's he's never known, the Terrell's, a family just as well off as his.

Little did he know he'd also find the woman of his dreams staying with them.

Allison is a beautiful young woman, but she's lost her memory, and has no idea how she got to Denver.

Nate and Allison share a tender bond as she regains her memory and he comes to terms with his new family.

They become each other's rocks, and soon they're falling in love.

But with a flood threatening to wipe out the whole family business, and a man who wants to eliminate Allison showing up on their doorstep, will their tender new love be able to bloom?

Or will it all fall apart before it's even properly begun?

Find out in this gripping yet heartfelt romance by Shanade White of BWWM Club.

Suitable for over 18s only due to sex scenes so hot, you'll be looking for your own handsome stranger.

## Get Free Romance eBooks!

Hi there. As a special thank you for buying this book, for a limited time I want to send you some great ebooks completely

**free of charge** directly to your email! You can get it by going to this page:

# www.afroromancebooks.com/physical

**These ebooks are so exclusive you can't even buy them**. When you download them I'll also send you updates when new books like this are available.

Again, that link is:

# www.afroromancebooks.com/physical

# Contents

## Prologue

Nate crept into the room and sat down in the chair next to his mother's bed not wanting to wake her. The nurse had told him on the way in that she'd just fallen asleep, these days sleep was a difficult thing to come by for his mother who was in the last stages of pancreatic cancer. The doctors had warned him the end would be especially hard to watch, but he'd been here every day since she'd been moved to hospice.

As he watched her, he thought about how much the disease had stolen from her. Her strength was only a part of what he missed, she rarely smiled these days. The pain, so intense at times he didn't know she stood it, but she hated the pain medication, said that it made her dopey. He hated to see her in so much pain, as much as he would miss her when she was gone, he would be relieved to know that she was finally at peace.

Settling back in the chair to wait, he thought about all the wonderful times he and his parents had shared over the years. He'd found thinking about the good times made it easier to keep a positive attitude around his mother. But looking at her now, her skin so pale he could almost see through it, and her body so wasted by the cancer it barely made a dent under the blankets, he knew it was only a matter of days before he'd be an orphan.

It was a strange way to look at himself since he was a 41 year old man, but none the less, once his mother was gone he'd be alone. His father had died almost five years ago and other than a few cousins he barely knew, there was no one else. He'd been married once, but that hadn't lasted long, she'd wanted a different life than he had, so they'd parted ways.

Since then he'd been involved with a few women, but those relationships had never felt quite right. He'd almost decided that he was ready to give up on romance completely, but there was a small part of him that still wanted to find the one woman who was perfect for him. She'd yet to appear, but then again he'd stopped looking for her, he'd just have to trust that fate would bring her to him.

His mother stirring in her bed interrupted his brooding thoughts, she opened her eyes and smiled when she saw him sitting there. "Hi." She said.

"Hi, Mom. You look good today." He said, smiling at her.

"That's a lie and you know it. But I love you for saying it."

"I love you too. Can I get you anything?"

"As a matter of fact there is something you can get me." She said, her voice breaking a little.

"Of course. What is it?"

"There's a photo album in the closet on the top shelf. Get it and bring it to me please." She said, pushing herself up a little in the bed.

Nate walked over to the closet and felt around on the top shelf. His hand brushed the album and he pulled it down. He'd never seen it before, but could tell that it was something his mother would have had. Taking it over to her, he gently set it on her lap then pulled up a chair, suddenly very curious about its contents.

"You've never seen this album before, it's one I kept only for myself, but it's time you saw it." She said, trying to pick it up and hand it back to him.

Nate grabbed the album before it hit the floor, picked it up and opened it. There on the front page was a wedding picture of two people he didn't recognize. Curious, he looked at his mother, waiting for an explanation. She gestured to him to keep looking, so he turned the page, then another and another, until he'd reached the end.

"Well?" She asked. "Do you recognize anyone?"

"Not really, but some of the men look familiar. Are they dad's relatives?" He asked, wondering why she'd kept this album a secret if it was of his father's family.

"Well, they are your father's family, but not the way you're thinking." His mother answered.

Confused by her cryptic answer, he paged through the book again. Suddenly he realized that the men in the picture looked like him, not his father, which was strange because he'd never met anyone in the family that looked like him. It had always been a bit of a joke with his cousins that he had actually been adopted, looking at these pictures made him wonder if it was true.

"Mom, what's going on? Who are these people?" He asked, suddenly very worried about what her answer would be.

"Son, I don't think there's any easy way to tell you this. I've been waiting for the right time and I'm afraid there isn't one." She said, then motioned for her water.

Nate helped her drink some water, his brain working overtime trying to figure out what she could have to tell him. Once he'd helped her settle back onto the pillow, he said. "Mom, what is it?"

"You know that you're father loved you more than anything in the world, but the truth is that he wasn't your biological father. I made a mistake many years ago, although seeing you sitting there, I question the use of the word mistake." She said, pausing to rest.

Nate stared at his mother, hardly believing what he'd heard. Looking down at the album again, then back up at his mother, he said, "Are you telling me that the man I knew as my father wasn't?"

"Yes, I'm sorry. I know this must be a shock to you, but I thought it was important you know. Once I'm gone you'll be alone in life and everyone needs a family. These people are your family, you have three brothers as well as a bunch of cousins." She said, a few tears rolling down her cheeks.

"Where are these people?" He asked.

"They have a ranch in Colorado. Your father's name is Jonathan Terrell, and you have three brothers, Garrett, Donovan, and Sebastian."

# Chapter 1

Allison closed the door on the last stall happy to be finished with the chore, cleaning stalls was never anyone's idea of fun, but she had to admit there was a feeling of satisfaction in seeing all the horses happy in their clean stalls. The truth was she didn't mind it all that much, it got her away from the house and the Terrell men, who were all home this weekend.

She found herself avoiding them whenever she possibly could, their mere presence making her nervous. But a lot of things made her nervous these days, which the doctors told her was only to be expected since she'd lost her memory. It didn't take a genius to figure out that what had happened to her had involved a man, probably one who looked a lot like the Terrell brothers.

It had been three weeks since she'd woken up in the hospital with no idea how she'd gotten there. As she'd laid there, trying to remember the events of the last few days, she realized she couldn't remember anything about her life. Panic had set in quickly and before she knew it she was having a full blown panic attack.

She must have cried out because the nurse had rushed in, at first relieved to see she was awake then concerned when she saw Allison's face. "What's wrong? Are you hurting somewhere?"

Allison tried to calm her breathing, this woman would know who she was. "I....I can't remember who I am or why I'm here." She said, her voice shaking.

The nurse looked at her for a second, then said, "You've had a head injury, it's not uncommon for your memory to be a little fuzzy. It should come back soon, just try to relax. I'll get the doctor since you're awake." She said, turning to leave the room.

"Where am I?" Allison begged before the nurse could leave.

"You're in Colorado, honey. I'll be right back, I promise."

The nurse returned before Allison could work herself into a panic again. "Well, it's good to see you awake. That's quite the nasty bump you had on your head. The nurse tells me your memory is a little fuzzy but I don't want you to worry, it's not uncommon with the kind of head injury you have."

Although that made her feel a little better she was still confused. "Do you know who I am? I must have had my purse or something with me."

"Well, when you were found there was no identification or cell phone with you. But the name Allison was engraved on your watch band so we're assuming that's your name."

"Something bad happened to me, but I can't remember anything." Allison said, suddenly panicking.

"You were hit over the head with a blunt object, it didn't puncture the skin, but you've sustained a minor brain injury. We've been able to figure out that you boarded a plane in Kentucky headed for Las Vegas, but you got off the plane in Denver. Airport security found you slumped over in a chair in baggage claim and called an ambulance which brought you here."

"How long ago?" She asked, not even sure what the date or the day of the week it was.

"You've been asleep for two days." The doctor said, as he cautiously began to examine her.

Allison fought down the panic, calming herself, trying to remember anything about her life. All that was there was a big blank and a feeling of impending doom. Somewhere deep down she knew she was in danger, but without her memory she had no idea from whom or what she'd been running.

With a gasp, she realized she'd been fleeing from someone when she'd gotten on that plane. "I was running from someone." She said, feeling a bit of hope that more would come back.

"Good, you're already getting memories back." The doctor said, writing in her chart. "But I want you to try and relax, physically you're in good shape but you still need to take it easy. I'm going to give you a light sedative to help you sleep."

Allison realized she was tired, sleep sounded like a good idea, the effort of trying to remember was draining her strength. She simply nodded and watched as the nurse injected the sedative into her IV line. Between the drug and her exhaustion, she was asleep in minutes, but before oblivion over took her, she saw a brief flash of green pastures with horses grazing in them. The memory left her feeling good, like she was seeing home.

When she'd woken the next time, the nurse was taking her vital signs, this time when she realized that her memory was blank the panic wasn't quite so bad. Seeing that she was awake, the nurse explained that a detective was waiting to talk to her if she felt up to it. Hoping that the detective might have more information, she gladly agreed.

But as it turned out, he didn't know much more than what the doctor had told her. "You got off the plane in Denver so there was no luggage we could match you to. They looked in Las Vegas and didn't find any there either. The airline employees who remembered you said that you seemed subdued but didn't seem debilitated in any other way. They had no idea that you were hurt."

"So, you have no idea who I am?" She asked, her stomach falling.

"I'm sorry but we don't. I'll keep working on your case but in the mean time we'll have to keep you safe because someone tried to hurt you." He said, patting her hand.

Allison wanted to burst into tears, she was stranded in Denver, no idea who she was and someone was trying to hurt her. "What am I going to do?" She said, barely containing her tears.

"I've been thinking about that and I think I have a solution that might be perfect for you. I have some friends that run a ranch in the mountains, they'd be happy to have you come stay with them for a while until you can get your memory back."

"They would take me in, knowing that I might be in danger?" She asked, wondering who these people were.

"When you meet them you'll understand why I want you there with them until we can get to the bottom of who you are and what happened to you. I know you don't know me, but trust me, the Terrell's will be able to help you and keep you safe at the same time."

Closing the door to the barn she had to admit that the doctor had been right, in the two weeks she'd been here they'd gone out of their way to help her. It seemed that each had a talent for helping and healing the wounded who seemed to find their way to the ranch high in the Colorado Mountains.

The only thing no one had been able to help her with so far, had been her memory.

She'd had flashes of people and places that must be a part of her past, but nothing that was coherent enough to help her in any way. The bits and pieces only made her more frustrated, especially the ones that came with a flash of emotion. It was like putting together a thousand piece puzzle without the box.

Scrunching down in her coat, she hurried across the yard to the house. Colorado in winter could be a harsh place, especially now in January when the snow was deep and the days short. But the lights were shining brightly in the main house, a sign that everyone was gathered together there again tonight. With a sigh, she braced herself for the commotion that would be found behind the door, it wasn't that she didn't like the Terrell's but when they were all together it could be overwhelming.

The first week she'd been here hadn't been that bad, Garrett and Sabrina had welcomed her with open arms, giving her a bedroom in the east wing of the house so she'd have plenty of privacy. But they'd also made sure she felt welcomed, Sabrina had invited her to help her with the therapy riders she had out to the ranch every day and Allison had found that she felt perfectly at home in the barn.

She'd instinctively known what to do with the horses and when Sabrina had suggested that she ride, it became obvious that horses had been a part of her past. By the end of the week it was clear that her life involved horses in some way, she'd become much too knowledgeable in a short time for it all to be new to her. Allison was relieved to be able to put some kind of story with a few of those flashes of memory, the pastures and horses she was constantly seeing made sense.

But now a week later, there had been nothing new, the same flashes that made little sense along with an overwhelming sense of doom, still plagued her. Now she'd have to deal with the entire Terrell clan who were all meeting here to go over the plans for Garrett and Sabrina's wedding which was only a few weeks away. She understood how important the occasion was for the family, but it was going to be a crazy few weeks, the house would be full of people, all of them new to Allison.

Luckily, Donovan and Sebastian had their own little cabins on the property so the nights would be quiet, at least until the wedding guests started arriving. Still she knew she was lucky to have found such a wonderful place to recover, and while overwhelming, everyone had been wonderful to her. Someday she'd find a way to pay them all back for their kindness, but that wasn't going to happen until she got her memory back.

When she walked into the kitchen, the entire family was gathered around Donovan and Elizabeth's little girl. Only six months old, she was already spoiled by everyone in the family. Allison had been given a brief description of her conception during a tumultuous time for the family when the former mayor of their town had tried to take Donovan and Terrell industries down.

She'd been told the story by Cinthia Terrell, proud mother of the three brothers. She and her husband Jonathan, had spent a quiet evening with her during her first week there when Garrett and Sabrina had been gone. Cinthia had spent the evening telling Allison about her son's wives and the peril they'd all gone through to find the love of their lives.

"It seems that the men of the family always have a way of finding their perfect mate, but it's never easy." Cinthia had said, a smile on her face. "It's all so romantic, don't you think?"

"I thought things like that only happened in books." Allison had said, laughing.

"Well, it's certainly been an exciting few years, but I suppose things will settle down now, after all our boys are all going to be married men once Garrett and Sabrina are married." She'd said, patting her husband's leg affectionately.

"Yes, but that just means more grandchildren." He'd said, then added. "I love girls but I'm hoping the next one will be a boy."

They'd all laughed and Allison had felt a moment of peace for the first time since she'd been released from the hospital. Since then she'd found her way to their house several times, finding some reassurance just being around Cinthia. It had been a place of calm when her fears had become overwhelming and panic threatened to take over.

Her entrance seemed to break the spell the baby had over everyone, they all turned to greet her, then went back to what they had been doing. Donovan took the baby from Elizabeth who joined Sabrina and Leslie in the kitchen. The trio of women were the other thing that had kept her sane over the last two weeks, it had been strange to find three African American women in the family, but thanks to them she didn't stick out like she'd feared she would.

It had also been a huge benefit that they, like herself, were more on the curvy side, she'd never considered herself overweight, but she filled out her clothes quite nicely. Finding clothes to wear had been a bit of a struggle at first, she'd had no idea what style she liked, so her one shopping trip had been a disaster. She'd arrived at the ranch with sweats and tee shirts unable to choose anything else.

They'd quickly taken her under their wing and into their closets, helping her remember that she loved jeans and button down shirts. It had been such a relief to finally remember something about the person she used to be that she'd even let them buy her a new pair of boots.

She washed her hands and joined the women in the kitchen, cooking it seemed was coming back as most other skills had, mostly unconsciously as she worked.

"Everyone all set in the barn?" Sabrina asked since Allison had been working in the therapy barn.

"Yep, all clean, fed, and happy."

"Thanks for doing that. I've got to find someone new to take over that barn. The kid I hired is good with the horses, but not so great at coming to work." She said, shaking her head.

"Why don't you hire me? I need something to keep me busy and then I could pay my own way while I'm staying here." She said, suddenly liking the idea.

"But I thought you liked working with the therapy patients, Leslie and I would miss your help." Sabrina said, looking to Leslie for affirmation.

"You're good with the kids and the horses." Leslie said.

"I could still do that, but this way I could contribute more. Don't think I don't appreciate everything you're doing for me, but I need to feel like I'm earning my own way." She said, then added. "Plus with the wedding, you won't have to worry about the horses at all. I'll handle everything."

"I for one think that's a fine idea." Garrett's booming voice made Allison cringe a little as he came into the kitchen.

"Well, since the master has spoken then I guess we have our new therapy hand." Sabrina said, laughing as she crossed the room to kiss Garrett.

Garrett seeing Allison's reaction to his voice, lowered it and asked, "When is dinner going to be ready?" Then added, "We're all starving, including the baby." When a high pitched wailing could be heard from the other room.

"I'll take care of that one ladies, the rest are up to you." Elizabeth said, leaving the room.

# Chapter 2

Nate's hands griped the wheel so tight his knuckles were turning white, he'd never imagined the Colorado Mountains would be so treacherous in the snow. The pictures he'd seen always showed the sun shining on the crystal white peaks, not a cloud in the sky, people in ski suits having fun. What they hadn't shown was the process of those peaks getting covered in snow.

He was experiencing it firsthand, and it wasn't much fun. Thankfully it was only a few more miles to the small resort town where his family lived. It was still strange to think of those people in the pictures as his family, but there was no denying it now. His mother had told him the whole story from the beginning to the end before she died. It had taken three long days for her to tell the story, during which time, he'd barley been able to sleep or eat.

They'd poured over the scrap book, which she'd kept hidden from both his father and himself for all these years. She'd explained that Jonathan Terrell had been her friend in college, they'd met through mutual friends and while not attracted to one another had become great friends.

"I never liked Jonathan that way. He was my friend and that was all. It was a bit unusual in those days, but perfectly harmless." She said, smiling at the memory.

"But something changed." Nate prompted her.

"Yes, when I met your father, I knew I'd met the man I wanted to marry. At almost the same time Jonathan met Cinthia and they were head over heels for each other. Strangely enough the four of us became a set, more or less became inseparable." She said, pointing to a picture of four young people their arms around one another.

"One night we'd all gone to a party together and things went crazy. Jonathan and Cinthia had been fighting because he wanted her to quit college and marry him right away. She wanted to finish and get her degree, but he wouldn't budge. They had a terrible fight and your father and I found ourselves in the middle. Before I knew it their fight had turned into ours and Jonathan and I were speeding away from the party in a cab."

Nate could already see where this was heading, but remained silent, waiting for his mother to go on. He could see that she was getting tired, but couldn't leave the story where she'd stopped. "What happened then?"

"I'm sure you can figure it out. It lasted for two weeks before I realized what I was doing and made up with your father and we were married right away. Jonathan too was shocked by our behavior and married Cinthia not long after that." She said, barely loud enough for him to hear.

He'd known what he was going to hear, but hearing it had still been difficult. No one wanted to think of their mother that way, especially with another man besides his father. But, at least now he knew the truth.

"I didn't know I was pregnant with you until after I married your father. For a while I hoped that you were really his, it could have been possible. But when you were born, supposedly a few weeks early, I knew that Jonathan was your father." His mother said, using her last bit of strength.

As much as he'd wanted to hear more, he'd know that it would have to wait for another day. He spent that night pacing around his house wondering if Jonathan Terrell or his father had known the truth. He was fairly sure that his father had never known, because if he had, he was sure they would have talked about it. The photo album gave him no clue whether or not Jonathan Terrell knew about him or not.

The next day, his mother had regained some of her strength and continued the story. "I never told anyone about your real parentage, it seemed like it would only cause pain. Your father was so happy to have you, and Jonathan was happily married and expecting his own baby, so I choose to keep it a secret." She said, watching for Nate's reaction.

"So Jonathan Terrell doesn't know I'm his son?" He asked, not sure how he felt about that.

"I think he always suspected, but I never told him outright. I think you're father knew as well, but he loved you as if you were his own. We never had any other children, so I think he was grateful to have you." She said, patting his hand.

"I never doubted that Dad loved me. But I can't see myself showing up on this man's doorstep out of the blue and announcing that I'm really his son, even if he might have some suspicion that I am." He said, his head spinning with all the implications.

"I'll leave that choice up to you. Jonathan knows you're my son, we've stayed in touch all these years, so a visit from you wouldn't be that surprising. What you tell him beyond that is up to you. I just wanted you to know the truth before I'm gone." She said, tears streaming down her face.

"Don't cry. I'm not upset. I've had two of the best parents a man could have asked for, you did what you did out of love." He said, drying his mother's tears.

It was only days after that when he lost her, the cancer finally winning the battle. After the funeral, he'd closed up both of their houses, taken a leave of absence from his job and set out for Colorado. Now thousands of miles later, and a hair raising trip up the mountain, he was finally in Pleasant Valley.

It was a charming town, clearly what they called a ski town, the resort could be seen from anywhere in the town. He'd booked himself a room at a local bed and breakfast, but only for one night. He wanted to get the lay of the land before he showed up at the Terrell ranch and announce his presence, still not sure what he was going to tell them when he did.

After he'd checked into his room and been fed a huge dinner, he collapsed into bed, too exhausted to worry about what might happen the next day. He awoke refreshed and after another huge meal, went out to explore the town. His first stop would have to be a store where he could purchase some cold weather gear. Living in Kentucky, he'd never had the need for anything more than a light jacket, but that certainly wouldn't cut it here.

Pleasant was a quaint little town, while it had the feel of a tourist town, it had managed to maintain some of its history. As an amateur architect he could see which of the buildings had been here the longest, and some of them had been here a long time. He'd parked his car in the center of town, thinking that he'd explore from the center out. When he found Main Street, his eyes greedily took in the old stone buildings, knowing that they had been standing for a hundred years or more.

He wandered up the street, shivering in his thin jacket, until he found a store with windows full of warm coats. He pushed his way through the doors, admiring the architecture of the old building when he got inside. At first he hardly noticed the group of women back in the corner laughing as they tried on hats. But, one of the women caught his eye, she was African America like her friends, but there was something different about her.

If his cop's instincts were right, she was in some kind of trouble. He recognized the way she carried her body, the way she kept scanning the store as if someone might be following her. He also recognized that she was very attractive, all curves and valleys, his idea of a real woman. Unlike most of his friends, he wanted nothing to do with the skinny women they all seemed to be constantly pursuing.

He wanted a woman he could wrap his arms around, a woman who wasn't so fragile he felt like he might break her. At a little over six feet tall and 200 pounds, those kind of women made him feel big and awkward. His thoughts were interrupted by the saleswoman, who'd seen him standing in the door way and had come bustling over.

"Hi, how can I help you today?" She said, stepping into his line of sight.

Forcing his thoughts from the woman across the room, he looked at the woman and said, "Well, first I need a much warmer coat. I've just come from Kentucky and I'm unprepared for this weather."

"I can help you with that. I'm Carrie Anderson. Have we met before?" She said, studying him.

"No, I've never been here. This is my first time in Pleasant Valley." He said, suddenly nervous under her scrutiny.

She shrugged her shoulders, "I'd swear we'd met before, but let's get you a new coat."

As she was showing him her selection of outerwear, the women made their way to the front carrying a pile of coats with them. They were laughing and chatting clearly having fun, his eyes were drawn once again to Allison, a fierce need to protect her washing over him. It was an irrational urge, considering he didn't know her, but he always trusted his instincts. He was about to go over to her, but the sales lady distracted him and when he looked back the women were gone.

*****

Allison hadn't missed the way Nate had been looking at her, she'd seen him the minute he walked through the door, his size alone capturing her attention. Knowing there might be someone out there trying to hurt her had made super conscious of her surroundings. But, strangely she'd found herself drawn to the huge man standing in the doorway. When the sales woman had pulled him to the back of the store, she'd watched him, wondering if she knew him, which could explain why she was drawn to him. But that couldn't be the case, if he knew her he would have said something.

As she walked out of the store with the other women, her new coat in bag, she shrugged off the encounter as simple physical attraction. Obviously that part of her brain was still working, but then it occurred to her that she might have a boyfriend or even a husband. She wasn't sure how old she was, but she was old enough for both. Thinking again of how much she didn't know about her own life started to depress her, so she pushed those thoughts aside and tried to have fun.

She'd been forced into the shopping trip, but had discovered that she'd enjoyed it, another new fact about herself she now knew. Each day she discovered something new about herself, and so far, she liked what she'd discovered. Now if she could only remember who she was, just her full name would be enough, maybe she could get all of her life back.

A few days later, they were all sitting down to dinner, Allison was still uncomfortable around the Terrell brothers, but they'd learned how to tone down their explosive personalities when she was around. She was still experiencing flashes of memory, but they were so brief that she still couldn't make sense of them. Everyone had been helping her try to piece them together when there was a knock at the door.

Daphne jumped up to answer it, a puzzled look on her face. She returned a few minutes later, still looking perplexed. "Jonathan there's a man at the front door looking for you. His name is Nate McAlister, he said he's the son of an old college friend of yours and that you'd know who he was." She said.

Allison could have sworn that Jonathan paled a little bit at the name, but he quickly covered his reaction with a cough and got to his feet. "I'd better see what this is all about." He said, pushing Daphne back into the dining room. "I'll be okay on my own."

Daphne sat back down at the table and looked at everyone as Jonathan left the room. They were all curious, but no one dared to say a word. Finally, Cinthia broke the silence. "Pass me some more of those potatoes they're really good."

\*\*\*\*\*

Nate stood in the entry way, looking at the fine construction of the house. He'd spent the last few days learning everything he could about the Terrell's and discovered that they had billions of dollars, but basically lived and worked like everyday people. The people of the town, had nothing but good things to say about them, singing their praises everywhere he turned.

He'd finally gotten up enough courage to drive up to the ranch and meet what he was finally beginning to believe was his other family. Knocking on the door had been one of the hardest things he'd ever done, now he was standing in the entry way feeling like he should just turn and flee. He'd almost made up his mind to do just that when an older man he recognized from the pictures came around the corner.

He stopped in his tracks and looked at Nate, then took a deep breath and let it out. "Son, I didn't know if you'd come, but I'm glad you have." He said, gesturing for Nate to follow him.

"My mother said I should, but now that I'm here I think this might be a mistake." He said, following Jonathan into what must be a library.

"Nonsense, your mother wrote to me and told me you'd be coming and I'm glad you have. It's time we got to know one another." Jonathan said, pouring them both a drink.

"But, you know...." Nate couldn't put it into words.

"That I'm your father? Yes, I've known for a long time. You look so much like my other boys it was obvious." Jonathan said, gesturing for Nate to sit in one of the chairs by the fire, which was burning pleasantly, warming the room against the cold outside.

Nate took a sip of his drink which was fixed just like he liked it. He had no idea what to say to this man who was his father. "I don't want to cause any trouble in your family." He finally said, knowing it to be true.

"My wife and I came to terms with the possibility that you were mine a long time ago, I couldn't hide my feelings from her. The rest of the family will understand eventually."

Nate had thought about this a lot, he hadn't planned to let Jonathan know who he was, but he certainly didn't want the rest of the family to know yet. "Would it be okay if you just introduced me as a friend of the family, I'd just be more comfortable with that for now."

"We can try, but eventually they're going to figure it out. Don't you think we should be open from the very beginning?" Jonathan said.

Nate considered his words, thinking about how it would look, him suddenly showing up and claiming a part of what they'd worked so hard to build. "No, I think it would be best if we all got to know each other first, I want them to understand that I'm not after anything but getting to know my family."

"You think they'll think you're after a cut of the family fortune. I can promise you that will be the last thing they'll think. But I'll honor you're wishes in this. This can't have been easy for you."

"It hasn't been. I feel like the life I thought I'd lived was all a lie, I just can't help it." Nate said, his emotions getting the better of him.

"I know son. Your mother wrote to me right before she passed and said that you were taking it hard since your father's gone as well. But I promise you it will get better, regardless of what you decide about telling the family, a stay at the ranch will make you feel better, it has that effect on people."

"Oh, I don't want to impose." Nate said, never imagining that they'd ask him to stay at the ranch.

"I insist. This is a huge house, plenty of room for another guest. I do have to warn you though, you've come to us just a week before Garrett's wedding." Jonathan said, shrugging his shoulders.

"Well, if you're sure it won't be an imposition I'd love to stay." Nate said, meaning it. Being this close to the family would help him make his decision.

"Come on I'll introduce you to the rest of the family. We were just finishing up dinner. Have you eaten? There's always plenty of food around here."

Suddenly Nate thought something about this whole experience felt right, the man walking next to him seemed familiar to him in some way. But those thoughts quickly fled when he walked into the room and saw the women who'd been in the store with him a few days ago. Seeing them lined up at the table, his heart sank, the woman he was so attracted to, was probably one of his brother's wives. That would be just his luck.

"Everyone, I'd like you to meet Nate McAlister. His mother was an old friend from college, she passed away recently and Nate decided he needed a change of scenery, so he's come for a visit." Jonathan said, capturing everyone's attention.

All eyes came to rest on Nate and he couldn't ignore the quick intake of breath from the older woman at the table. He assumed that this was Cinthia, Jonathan's wife and his step-mother. She recovered quickly and pasted a smile on her face, but he could see that it was difficult for her. Jonathan might have been overstating how resigned she was to the situation, since she obviously knew who he was.

The rest of the family didn't seem to notice not only her reaction but how much he looked like the three Terrell brothers. One of the younger women, who looked a lot like the Terrell's jumped to her feet. "Come and sit down. Would you like something to eat? We're just about to have coffee and desert or I could make you a plate."

Nate sat down in the chair she got for him, feeling a little overwhelmed, "I would love to join you for desert." He said, remembering his manners even though his heart was pounding in his chest.

Once Daphne, with the help of the other women, had served them all, she began to introduce everyone. It was hard to keep track of who everyone was, but when she came to Allison he paid special attention, relieved when he discovered that she was a guest here as well and not married to one of his brothers. After introductions were made the conversation strayed back to the wedding which was only a week away.

He gathered from the talk that it was to be a huge celebration, a good excuse to throw off some of the winter blues he understood were so common during the winter here. Nate was content to sit and listen, learning a lot about his family just from listening. He was also trying to figure out how to talk to Allison, who certainly hadn't escaped his attention. She too was sitting quietly, listening to the conversation, but he could sense that she was only partly there, her mind wandering.

Allison was trying to study Nate, the man she'd seen in the store, but every time she looked at him, he was looking at her. It was a strange coincidence that he'd shown up here, an old friend of the family. But, Jonathan seemed to know who he was, so she shouldn't be so wary of his presence. But, as she continued to watch him, she realized that her discomfort wasn't because she was afraid, it was because she was attracted to him.

Right now she had no business being attracted to anyone, especially when she didn't know who might be out there looking for her. She kept hoping that one morning she'd wake up and figure out who she was, where she belonged and finally be able to go home. A romance was the last thing she needed right now. But, there was no doubt that Nate was a very attractive man, probably way out of her league as well, since men like him usually went for skinny blonde women.

When they all got up to move to the living room, Sabrina and Daphne dragging their wedding plans with them, Nate chose the seat closest to Allison's and sat down. "What brings you to the ranch?" He asked, not realizing what a difficult question he'd just asked her.

## Chapter 3

Allison hesitated for so long, Nate realized that he'd asked a question she didn't want to answer. So he quickly covered his mistake, "I could use another cup of coffee. Want to join me?" He said, getting to his feet and holding out his hand to help Allison up.

She looked around the room and seeing that the family was deep in conversation about the wedding, decided it would be okay for them to slip out. Frankly she was relieved to be out of the crowded room and gladly took Nate's hand. When she did, a strange pulse of electricity seemed to travel from his hand to hers. Shocked, she looked at their joined hands, then up at Nate, who must have felt it too.

When their eyes met, he smiled at her, making her stomach flutter with attraction. Embarrassed, she looked down, but not before she saw the attraction in his eyes as well. Nate pulled her to her feet, but held onto her hand until they were in the kitchen. It felt nice to have her hand in his, a warm rush of contentment washed over her, which was strange since she hardly knew the man.

He poured them both a cup of coffee, then moved to the side so she could add cream and sugar to hers. Leaning up against the counter, Nate took a sip from his cup then said, "I guess I should have called ahead instead of just showing up here."

"Honestly, I don't think they mind. There's always a crowd around here, but at night everyone goes home. You'll see, it will quiet down, at least until the wedding guests start arriving." Allison said.

"I hope I'm not over stepping my bounds, they might not have room for me. I should probably just stay in town." Nate said, again questioning the decision to stay at the ranch.

"There's plenty of room. It may not look like it, but this house is really big. I'm staying in the east wing alone right now. I could give you a quick tour if you like, I don't think Sabrina would mind." Allison offered, stepping away from the counter.

"That's okay, but maybe we could find someplace quiet to sit. I'm not quite up to listening to any more wedding plans."

"Typical man." Allison said, laughing, something she hadn't been doing much lately. "We can sit in the sunroom, it's my favorite room in the whole house. Come on, it's this way."

Nate followed Allison, thinking how much he'd like to kiss her. Then was shocked at himself for the thought, but she was a very attractive woman. He'd never been attracted to a black woman before, but there was something about Allison that drew him to her. It wasn't just the feeling that she needed help that had raised his interest, it was more than that, what he wasn't sure.

Allison suddenly found herself as nervous as if she was on a first date, which was silly since Nate was just another lost soul who had found his way to the Terrell's front door. When they walked through the door of the sunroom, he could understand why Allison loved it so much. The huge windows would let in the sunlight even on the coldest of days, and now when it was dark, the stars were glinting magically in the sky.

There was a fire burning in the huge fireplace making the room warm and cozy, so Nate steered her toward the couch that faced the fireplace, and together they sat down. There were several moments of silence, each of them trying to calm the attraction they were feeling. Allison, unsure of the wisdom of letting her attraction go any farther and Nate, shocked that this woman was suddenly in his life.

"So tell me." Nate said, breaking the silence. "Where is this wedding going to be held?"

"It's the craziest thing, they're going to have it out in one of the pastures." She said, shaking her head.

"It's the middle of the winter in Colorado. Everyone is going to freeze." He said, shivering even thinking about it.

"Well, they've got tents and heaters and they insist it won't be that cold."

"Hmm, maybe I better go back to that outerwear store in town before the wedding." He said, rubbing his hands together.

"I thought that was you I saw the other day."

"I left Kentucky with no idea of how cold it was actually going to be here. A coat was the first item on my list that day." He said, laughing.

Allison had a moment of panic when she heard he was from Kentucky, but reminded herself that he was a friend of the family not someone looking for her. Nate noticed her silence and how stiff she'd just gotten.

"I'm sorry. Did I say something wrong?" He asked, concerned.

"No, it's just that......" She had no idea how to even begin her story. "You're from Kentucky?" She asked instead.

"Yeah, from a little town in the north, but I've been in the city for a long time. I'm a detective on the police force, have been for almost twenty years."

Allison immediately relaxed, this man was safe, her inter-voice shouted at her in relief. Nate wasn't sure what he'd said that reassured her, but he could feel Allison relax, and continued. "I lost my mother recently and needed to get away."

"I'm sorry to hear that. Is your dad still alive?" She asked, wondering if she had a mother and father and if so why they weren't looking for her.

"No, I lost him five years ago, they were my only family. After my mom's funeral, I just couldn't handle being there alone, so I packed up and headed here." Nate said, hoping that if he trusted her with his secrets she'd trust him with hers.

Before she could stop herself Allison said, "I wish I knew where my parents were." Then covered her mouth with her hand.

"Your parents are missing?"

"No, I don't even know if I have any parents." Allison couldn't stop the tears from rolling down her cheeks.

Nate put his arm around her and pulled her close. "Tell me what's wrong. I know that you're afraid of something, maybe I can help."

Allison pulled herself together, then said, "Something happened to me, maybe in Kentucky, but I'm not sure. I woke up here in Denver in the hospital with a brain injury and no memory of my life. The only reason we even know that my name is Allison is because it was engraved on a watch I was wearing."

"Oh, sweetheart, I had no idea it was that bad." Nate said, suddenly very angry that someone had hurt this woman.

"I don't know how old I am. I don't know if I have any family. I don't even know if I'm married or involved with someone. It's driving me crazy, but the more I try to remember the fuzzier things get." She said, sobbing with relief to finally talk about how she was feeling.

Nate let her cry for a few minutes, making reassuring noises but not saying a word. When she'd finally drained the worst of her emotion, he said, "Tell me what you do know."

Allison took a deep breath and told him what she did remember, including the memory flashes and what she thought they meant. As she talked, a terrible thought occurred to her, "I think that the reason we still don't know who I am is because no one is looking for me." She said, her voice trembling to think that she might be alone in the world with no one to even miss her.

"I'm sorry to say that I thought that too. Would you mind if I got in touch with the detective who is working your case? If this whole thing started out in Kentucky, I might be able to help from that end." Nate said, his mind already beginning to work the crime.

"That would be so nice of you. I don't know how much longer I can go on looking over my shoulder for someone I won't even recognize, wondering who I am and where I belong. It's exhausting." She said, taking a deep soothing breath. "The Terrell's have been wonderful to me, but it's been almost a month and I've had nothing but flashes."

"What do the doctors say?"

"That I've been through a trauma so terrible that my brain is blocking it and everything else out. They think that it's because it involves someone in my life I thought I could trust or something along those lines. The memories will come back eventually, they claim, either when something triggers them or when I feel safe enough to face what happened."

Nate was quiet for a while, thinking about this. "It makes sense, but I'm still going to try and find out who you are." He said, with determination. He wanted this woman more than he'd ever wanted any other, but until they sorted out who she was it would be unfair to pursue her romantically. They could both end up in a world of hurt if she regained her memory and was already involved or even worse married.

"Thank you." Allison said, something telling her that putting her trust in Nate would be one of the best decisions she'd ever made.

They sat quietly for a few minutes, but that quiet was disrupted by the sound of the family breaking up their meeting. Sebastian found them in the sunroom, insisting that he'd drive Nate back to town to pick up his things, Nate argued at first but when Sebastian pointed to the snow that had been falling for the last hour, he had to agree.

"I swear the stars were out just a little while ago." He said, shaking his head. "I'll take you up on that offer, I'm not all that good at driving in this stuff yet."

"You're going to discover that the weather here can change in the blink of an eye, especially up here in the mountains. We've already had a record amount of snow this year and the real snow hasn't even started to fall."

"Guess I better buy those boots I saw in town as well as some more cold weather gear." Nate said, with a smile.

"I'd strongly recommend it, brother." Sebastian said.

Nate was a little shocked when Sebastian called him brother, but realized that he was just using a figure of speech. Breathing a sigh of relief, he got up and followed Sebastian out of the room, then stepped back in and said, "I'll see you in the morning Allison. Sleep well, we've got work to do tomorrow."

Allison felt a little thrill of anticipation to know Nate would be here in the morning when she woke up. It had been so long since she'd had anything other than working with the horses to look forward to. She went to bed smiling for the first time since she'd woken up in the hospital. Not only would Nate be helping her find out who she was, he was an extremely attractive man, who if she wasn't mistaken, was attracted to her too.

In the morning at breakfast only Garrett, Sabrina and their two children, Maria and Scott were there. Allison liked breakfast for this reason, it was the only quiet time of the day, the kids providing just enough entertainment that early in the day. She was just finishing her second cup of coffee, finally ready to face the day when Garrett cleared his throat.

"Nate, Sebastian tells me that you're a detective." He said, turning serious.

"Yes, twenty years on the force." Nate said, wondering where this was going.

"Well, with Allison's permission I'd like to ask you a favor." Garrett said, looking to Allison.

"I've already told him about my memory loss. He's offered to help if he can." She said, smiling shyly at Nate.

"Good, just let me know what you need and I'll make sure you have it. Take over the library if you want, then you'll have some quiet and you'll be away from the mess." Garrett said, gesturing to the piles of wedding stuff everywhere.

"That sound like a plan. I just need an internet connection and I'm good to go. I've got my laptop with me so I can get started right away." Nate said, getting to his feet, as anxious as ever to solve a problem.

"Allison and I have riders coming out this morning, then I've got errands to run for the wedding." Sabrina said, kissing Garrett on her way to the sink. "Esmerelda is going to be out this week to help around the house, so don't be surprised if she's underfoot all week."

"I'll get Nate set up in the library and then I better see how the prep work on the pasture is going. They should be delivering the tents and heaters later today." Garrett said, getting to his feet as well.

Allison followed Sabrina out to the barn feeling positive that Nate would be able to get some results. "Nate seems like a nice guy." Sabrina said, not having missed the electricity sparking between them.

"I'm so happy he's going to help. He's from Kentucky. Did you know that?"

"I thought that's what I heard. If you're from Kentucky that might be a big help. It's funny, he reminds me of someone but I can't figure out who." Sabrina said, a furrow creasing her brow.

"I kind of thought that he looked like Garrett, but I don't know, maybe it's just because they're both dark and about the same age." Allison said, thinking about how much the two men looked alike.

"Hmm, I don't know." Sabrina said, then was distracted by their first student of the day, a young man who had been in a car accident and was learning to walk again. Leslie would be working with him later as well, but first he'd ride.

Allison tried to keep her mind off what Nate might be discovering about her life, but by lunch she was too curious to wait any longer. As soon as she came into the house, she went straight to the library to see if he had any information for her. He was on the phone when she walked into the room, which gave her a chance to watch him.

He'd obviously been running his fingers through his hair, it was sticking up at strange angles all over his head. His forehead was creased and he was writing something down on a notebook in front of him. When he saw her standing there, a huge smile broke out on his face and she couldn't help but smile back at him.

She came farther into the room and sat down in one of the chairs facing the desk. When he finished the call, he shook his head no to her silent question. "I'm afraid I don't have any news for you yet. I've made contact with several departments in my area, but it's going to take some time to contact them all.

At this point, I'm just hoping I'll get lucky and come across someone who knows something."

"That's okay, I know it's not going to be that easy or the local police would have figured out who I am by now. Thank you for trying though." She said, sitting back in the chair.

"I'm not giving up yet. There's still lots of avenues to explore." Nate said, getting up from the chair. "I'm starving, let's go find some lunch."

"Okay." Allison said, knowing that she had been hoping for too much too soon.

Seeing her dejected face, Nate couldn't help but put his arm around her and giving her a gentle squeeze. He said, "Don't worry I'll figure it out. I'm a very good detective."

Allison gave him the best smile she could muster, then said, "I know I'm being impatient but it's just hard." She wanted to add, especially not knowing if I can go with my attraction to you or not.

Nate went back to work after lunch, which left Allison on her own, instead of hovering over his shoulder, she decided it was time to pay a visit to Cinthia, who was home working on wedding preparations and would probably love some company. It always made Allison feel better when she spent time with Cinthia.

For several days, life followed the same pattern, riding in the morning and afternoons spent with the family, which was growing larger and larger as the big day approached. She and Nate had been enjoying the quiet of the east wing alone, but as family arrived, the bedrooms quickly began to fill up. They had begun the habit of sneaking off to the sunroom after dinner, using the excuse that Nate needed to fill her in on the progress of his investigation, but the truth was Nate realized Allison needed some quiet time.

They were sitting by the fire on the couch they always occupied when Nate brought up the subject of missing person's reports. "I've talked to every law enforcement agency in Kentucky and the surrounding areas, no one has made a missing person's report for anyone matching your description."

"I guess that means that no one is looking for me." She said, suddenly feeling very alone.

"Not necessarily, I think it means you don't have a significant other, but that doesn't mean that you don't have any friends or family."

"But wouldn't they be looking for me?" She asked, still confused about how someone could just disappear and no one noticed.

"Well, they could have been thrown off by a well-placed lie or two. I think we just need to wait and see what turns up, I've put just about every cop in a four state area on the case so something will come up."

"Nate, I really appreciate everything you're doing for me. I can't tell you how much better I feel knowing that you're on the case." Allison said, looking into his eyes, something she'd been avoiding the last few days, unsure of her feelings.

"I know I shouldn't say this because it's completely selfish, but I'm glad I haven't found a husband or boyfriend out there looking for you." He said, sliding closer to her on the couch.

"What?" She asked, confused.

"Well, the thing is I've been wanting to kiss you for days, but with not knowing who might be out there I've been resisting. But now, I don't see any reason to." He said, cupping her face with one hand.

Allison was lost in his blue eyes, a blue so startling that it took her breath away. She didn't remember his eyes being that blue before and with a shock realized that it was desire making them that color. It was all there to see, and a delightful shiver ran thought her body. Knowing that it was probably a mistake she leaned into him, giving him all the permission he needed to kiss her.

When his lips came down on hers, it was like a bolt of lightning went through her body, every nerve suddenly alive and vibrating. What had at first been a gentle kiss, turned urgent almost immediately, Allison pouring all her despair and heartbreak into the kiss, Nate feeling like he'd never kissed a woman before.

Her body on fire, she wrapped her arms around him, loving the feel of his hard body pressed up against hers. Before she knew it his hand was under her shirt and he'd found one of her breasts, the feeling of his hand driving her desire higher, making coherent thoughts difficult. A part of her knew that it was much too soon for this, but another part telling her that there was something right about being in Nate's arms.

Before things could go any farther, they heard footsteps coming down the hallway and quickly parted, both panting a little from the encounter. Allison's face was flushed with desire when Sabrina poked her head in the door, she couldn't hide the smile that appeared when she realized she'd interrupted something.

"Sorry, I just wanted to tell you guys we're having desert now." She said, then turned and fled the room.

Nate looked at Allison, "I'm sorry I shouldn't have done that, I didn't mean to get that carried away."

"I wanted you to, I've been wanting that since I saw you in the store that first time. But Nate what if there is someone out there looking for me, aren't we playing with fire?" She said, feeling guilty for no reason.

"If there was someone out there looking for you, they would have found you by now." He said, pulling her to him.

She listened to his heart beating, taking strength from him, hoping that he was right because no matter who she was, she really liked this man. She did wonder why he didn't have a significant other, after all he seemed like the whole package. If she was going to become involved with him, she really needed to find out more about him, but first she wanted desert.

## Chapter 4

The morning of the wedding the sun was shining and there was no snow in the forecast, it would be a busy day preparing for the wedding, but Allison was actually looking forward to the night. Things had been so hectic the last few days that she'd had little time alone with Nate and none of that time had included another kiss. She was afraid that he'd changed his mind about her, getting involved with someone who didn't know who they were was a little dangerous.

But any doubts she had were soon erased when he knocked on her door to take her to the wedding that night. She'd chosen a sweater dress that showed off every curve, it was made from the softest yarn in a shade of cream that accentuated her caramel colored skin. She'd put her long hair up on top of her head, and brushed on some makeup, then finally dabbed on some perfume.

"You look fantastic." Nate said, pulling her to him and kissing her. "And you smell just as good."

The kiss was so sudden, it took her breath away, but kissing him was just as wonderful as she remembered. When the kiss was over, Nate ran his hands up and down her hips, sending shivers of desire radiating out from her core. "Mmm, you're just as soft as I'd imagined." He whispered in her ear, increasing that desire even more.

"It's the yarn in my dress." She said, looking up at him, hoping his hands wouldn't stop.

"No, it's definitely you." He said, bending down for another kiss.

Allison might have just let him push her back into the room at that point, but luckily for both of them, someone opened a door down the hallway. "We'd better get going, the wedding starts soon." Allison said, grabbing her wrap off a hook by the door.

"Yes, I suppose we better, otherwise I'm going to drag you into your room and...." His words trailed off as they were joined by another couple.

Allison couldn't help but giggle, another second and Nate would have embarrassed them both. Nate offered her his arm, and together they walked down the stairs. The house was strangely quiet, but since the wedding was about to begin it made sense that everyone would be out of the house. When they came out of the front door there was a sled waiting to take them down to the wedding, Allison didn't think she'd even been in a more romantic setting.

She thought that the wedding would be a wonderful experience, but as soon as the ceremony started, she began having flashes of another wedding. Along with these flashes came an impending sense of doom. If she'd been able to leave without making a scene she would have, but instead she sat stiffly gripping the sides of her chair as the flashes bombarded her with information.

Nate could sense her discomfort and took one of her cold hands in his, he gestured to her asking if she needed to leave, but she shook her head no. She held onto his hand, feeling better for the connection, but as soon as the ceremony was over, he ushered her out of the tent.

"What happened in there? You remembered something, didn't you?" Nate asked, guiding her to one of the barns so they'd be out of the cold.

"I keep getting flashes of another wedding, the woman is older and the man is much younger. Every time I see them,

I feel a sense of doom, a sense of knowing that it's all wrong. I'm sorry I ruined the wedding for you. We should go back, I'll be okay." She said, forcing a smile.

"I'm sorry this is upsetting you, but it is encouraging that you've remembered something. We don't have to go back if it's going to be difficult for you." He said, pulling her into his arms.

"As long as you're with me, I'll be okay." She said, reassured by the sound of his heart beat.

"If you want to leave, tell me and we're out of there." He said, taking her hand to help her back to the wedding festivities.

Allison was on edge for the rest of the night, images of the other wedding flashing through her mind. She made it through dinner, but as the dancing began she began to feel panic setting in. The images in her mind becoming clearer as the night continued. Finally, she couldn't hide her anxiety from Nate any longer.

"I think it's time to leave." He said, looking at her hands clenched in her lap.

"I'm ready, but won't it be rude to leave so early?" She said, hoping he'd say no.

"I think Garrett and Sabrina would understand. Besides, I don't think we'll be missed." He said, helping her to her feet.

When they got back to the house Nate wasn't sure how to proceed. "Do you want to talk about what you've been remembering? I don't want to push you, but it might be good to talk about it when it's still fresh in your mind."

"Honestly, I'd rather think of something else right now. I don't think I'll forget what I've seen." She said, shivering at the memories and their effect on her.

Nate pulled her into his arms and kissed her, then said, "Did that help?"

"Mmm, definitely. But Nate I still think this isn't a good idea. You don't even know who I am. I could be a criminal for all you know." She said, pulling away and looking up at him. Her attraction to Nate was so strong she knew she wouldn't be able to resist him if he pushed her.

"I seriously doubt you're a criminal. I'm a pretty good judge of character. I promise we won't do anything you don't want to do." He said, leading her to the sunroom, where a fire was still burning.

Allison knew deep down that she could trust Nate, it made no sense, but it was the one thing in her life that she was sure of. Sitting down on the couch, she let Nate pull her into his arms. They sat in silence for a long time, content to be where they were. But, Allison could feel the tension building between them, she wanted him to kiss her more than anything else right now.

When she was in his arms, she could forget about her problems and just live in the moment. It was probably a mistake she would live to regret, but she was completely infatuated with Nate and wanted him to take that closeness to the next level. She'd never be the one to initiate anything, but if he did, she had every intention of taking advantage of it.

She didn't have to wait very long for Nate to make his move, he'd been sitting next to her thinking about what he might find under her dress. Then feeling guilty for taking advantage of her when she was so terribly wounded, but one thing he was sure of was that he wanted her. It was wrong, but he wanted her more than he'd ever wanted a woman in his life.

He could sense the tension between them and knew that she wanted him just as much, but taking that next step would be a huge decision, one that might change both of their lives. He had no idea why he thought that but knew somewhere deep down that it was true. Waiting until she knew who she was might have been the logical approach to the situation, but right now he wasn't thinking very logically.

Deciding to trust his instincts, he turned to Allison and took her face in his hands, then lowered his mouth to hers in a kiss that only left her wanting more. Allison wrapped her arms around him, then threaded her fingers though his hair, something she'd been wanting to do for a long time, and brought his head down for another kiss.

He wanted nothing more than to lose himself in Allison, her body was pressed up against his, her breasts pressed seductively against his chest. Panting with desire, he broke the kiss. "Are you sure about this. I don't want to take advantage of you when you're so fragile." He said, stroking her cheek with the back of his hand.

"I'm not that fragile, besides I am a grown woman. I trust you Nate and I want this as much as you do." She said, kissing the center of his palm.

That one kiss was all it took to drive him past the edge of reason, forgetting any reservation he'd had, he took her hand and pulled her up off the couch. They mounted the stairs in silence, each a little nervous about what was about to happen. Allison was sure she'd had sex before, but couldn't honestly remember it.

She was probably crazy to be doing this, but it was time to start her life again, if she never remembered who she was then she'd start a new life. That thought actually made her feel better, after all she had a place to live and people who cared for her here. It was a place to start, and so was Nate. He was a place to start her new life.

When they got to the door of her room, Nate stopped and took both her hands in his. "Are you sure?" He asked again.

"Yes, I'm sure. Nate, it's been over a month and I haven't gotten my memory back. I've been afraid to face the idea that I might never get it back, but it is a possibility."

"Allison, we'll figure this out." He said, "Don't give up."

"I'm not giving up. I'm just being practical. It's time to get on with life, every day I spend living in a past I can't remember, is another day I've lost. I just realized I'm tired of living that way. I'm going to start living my life in the here and now. I'm in a safe place with people who care, it's time to figure out where I'm going to go from here." She said, feeling stronger by the minute.

"I hope I'm in those plans somewhere." Nate said, suddenly afraid she'd changed her mind about him. It was strange to feel so exposed with a woman, but he knew he'd be devastated if she turned away from him now.

"You are definitely part of those plans. I'm going to start living life tonight with you." She said, suddenly embarrassed by her bold words.

"That's the best thing I've heard all day." He said, pulling her into his arms and kissing her.

Her room, like many of the other, had a fireplace in it. She was in no hurry to rush what was about to happen, she wanted to take her time and enjoy it. "Would you start a fire, it's a little chilly in here?"

Nate was a little disappointed that she seemed to be pulling away, but agreed. He'd let her set the pace, and if nothing happened he'd be satisfied with that as well. He was in this for the long haul, it felt like Allison had made a major breakthrough tonight. Making the decision to move on with her life, accepting the possibility that the void would be permanent had taken a lot of strength. Not only was he proud of her, but he was happy to see her inner strength returning.

"I'm going to change out of this dress, as much as I love it, it cost a fortune and I'd hate to ruin it." She stammered, thinking of the silky nightgown and robe she was planning to put on.

"I'll go get us something to drink." Nate said, sensing her nervousness and wanting to give her some space.

When he returned a few minutes later, a bottle of champagne in hand she was still in the bathroom. He took off his jacket, tie and shoes, then made himself comfortable on the couch. When he heard the bathroom door open, he jumped to his feet, wanting to reassure Allison. But when he saw her framed in the door, the bathroom light behind her, thoughts about anything but how beautiful she was ceased to exist in his mind.

He crossed the room in several long strides and took her in his arms, his mouth coming down on hers in a heated kiss that had her knees buckling from the intensity. When they finally had to pause for breath, Nate looked into her eyes and said, "I want you Allison, more than I've ever wanted a woman. It's been driving me crazy for days. Every time I look at you I imagine us together."

Allison felt all her breath whoosh out of her, his words creating a storm of desire inside her. His words had taken her from mild excitement straight to full blown desire. "I want you too Nate, but I'm a little nervous, I can't remember doing this before." She finally admitted, breathless with wanting him.

"We can take it slow." He said, pulling her over to the bed and sitting her down.

"Okay." She said, suddenly shy.

Nate knew he needed to take his time, but every time he touched her, his desire was like a fire rushing though him. But, he'd go as slowly as she needed, taking his time wouldn't be the end of the world. Nate took her hand and kissed the palm, then trailed kisses up the inside of her arm sending delicious waves of pleasure washing over her.

When he reached her neck, she bent her head back, loving the goosebumps that erupted as he nuzzled her neck. "You smell like almonds and vanilla." He said, making her laugh.

"So I'm a cookie?" She asked.

"Mmm, a very yummy cookie." He said, finding her mouth with his.

Allison relaxed into his arms, lost in a fury of desire mixed with pleasure, enjoying the kiss but wanting more. Nate sensed her need, found her breast with his hand, while he wrapped the other in her hair, pulling her closer to him. Allison was moaning in her throat, his hand massaging her swollen breast sending waves of pleasure through her. When his finger and thumb found her breast and worked the hard peak between them. She broke the kiss, no longer able to breathe.

Nate bent his head down and captured that same peak in his mouth through the silk of her nightgown, making her lean back on the bed. His hand strayed down her legs and lifted the hem of her nightgown up, exposing her legs to his roaming hands. When his hands pushed her legs apart she could feel the cold air on her exposed sex which was hot and dripping already.

A low growl in Nate's throat made Allison smile when he discovered she was naked underneath the nightgown. His hand traced a path from the center of her thigh, up to the juncture of her thighs then with one finger his found her clit and began to stroke her. Allison's body responded to his touch, her orgasm rocking through her so quickly she couldn't breathe for long seconds. Nate wanted nothing more than to bury his swollen length inside her, but knew that she still wasn't ready. Standing, he stripped off his clothes, then removed her night clothes, his eyes never leaving hers.

Allison scooted up to the top of the bed, her legs still shaking from the force of her orgasm, but her body still wanting more. Nate laid down beside her and pulled her into his arms, his mouth finding hers in a searing kiss. The feel of his naked body pressing against hers, his erection throbbing against her leg, had Allison squirming against him.

He rolled her onto her back and spread her legs again, his mouth leaving hers to suckle on her breasts, which were swollen and sensitive to every lick, bite, and touch. Allison bravely found his erection and stroked him, loving the sounds that came from deep in his throat. His finger found her core and he began to stroke her, driving her nearly to the edge again.

He stopped just as she felt her orgasm cresting, then positioned himself between her legs and drove himself inside her, gasping with relief to finally be inside her. Nothing had ever felt so right in his entire life, he felt like he'd finally found the place where he belonged. With a feeling of possession he'd never felt before, he drove himself into her over and over, forever branding her as his.

Allison was lost in a storm of sensation, sure that nothing had ever felt like this before. The feeling of Nate so deep inside her, joined to her in this most intimate of acts felt right to her. Deep in her soul she knew that this was supposed to happen, that she was meant to be with this man who had saved her from a life of despair and doubt.

Their orgasms came rushing over them at the same time, Allison's body clenching around Nate's as the rest of the world ceased to exist. Nate collapsed on top of Allison unable to move for long minutes, finally he managed to roll onto his back, taking her with him. She laid her head on his chest, listening to the sound of his heart beat, thinking that if this was all her life had to offer, she'd be just fine.

Nate was beyond happy at that moment but knew that life would intrude on them all too soon. He hated to bring the topic up, but he wanted to know what she'd remembered during the wedding earlier that night. "I hate to ruin the mood, but I was wondering what it was that you remembered earlier tonight." He said, rubbing her back.

"It was just a bunch of flashes of a wedding. I think it was my mother and she was marrying a much younger man, who I'm sure I didn't like. Then there were a bunch of flashes of him in what looked like a barn, he was yelling and I felt scared." She said, shivering at the memory.

"That seems like progress to me." He said, afraid to push her any further.

"Do you think that he's the man that hurt me? I feel like he was about my age, I also feel like he was bad to my mother in some way. The worst part is some part of me thinks that my mother is gone. That she died." Allison said, close to tears.

"It's okay, I'm here." Nate said, "Don't try to force it. Give it some time, it's coming back."

Allison took a deep breath, "It's all there, I can feel it but I'm afraid to let it out. I know there's something bad just waiting for me."

"I know but, I'll be right here with you when it all comes back. Nothing that you remember is going to chase me away." He said, leaning up on one elbow to kiss her, then added. "Remember that you're safe here with me and the Terrell's, we'll protect you."

Nate's words calmed her, no matter what the threat, she knew she had people who would see that she was safe. "I know and I'm grateful, but I still worry that something terrible is waiting for me when my memory returns." She said, taking a deep breath.

"Whatever it is, we'll handle it together." Nate said, "In case you haven't noticed, I'm very protective of the people I care about and I already care a lot about you Allison."

Her heart just about melted hearing his words, there was a certain amount of relief to hear that he cared about her, after all they'd moved so fast in their relationship, a part of her worried that he was just out for some easy sex. But seeing the look in his eyes, her worries evaporated, no man could fake the intensity she found there.

"Will you stay here with me tonight? I don't want to be alone." Allison said, suddenly feeling very vulnerable.

"There is nothing in this world that could get me to leave your bed tonight. Except maybe to get that bottle of champagne I brought up." He said, sliding out of bed and coming back with the bottle and two glasses.

He poured them each a glass then handed her one, she took a sip, then laughed when the bubbles tickled her nose. "I don't think I've ever had champagne before." She said.

"Well, there's always a first time for everything." He said, then took the glass from her hand and set it on the nightstand. He gathered her into his arms, "But I also think second times can be pretty great too."

His hands had begun to roam over her body, "Hmm, I'm not sure about that, maybe you should show me." She said, feeling brave.

"I can do that." He said, his finger sliding inside her to find that she was already wet and ready for him.

# Chapter 5

As the truck bounced along the rutted dirt road, Matt was dreaming of not only fame but the money winning the Triple Crown would bring him. He'd worked hard to get to this point, done anything it took to see his dream fulfilled. If he'd stepped on a few toes in the process so be it, after all only the strong survived, and he was one of the strong.

He'd made a life of finding people who weren't strong and taken advantage of them in any way possible. It had always worked in the past and his latest scheme was no different. He'd been working on this one for four long years not including the time it took to set the whole thing up. Barbra Stevens had been an easy target, a woman who was facing the end of her life, looking for someone to make her feel young again.

It had been perfect, not only was she vulnerable, but she owned a prime horse breeding farm. Every con he'd ever run had been leading up to this one big score and Barbra had made it easy for him. The only snag had been her daughter, only a few years younger than him, she'd been suspicious from the moment he'd set foot on the property.

Nothing he'd tried had altered that distrust especially after he married her mother, but he had to admit that Allison had been right about him. He had to give her some credit for that, it hadn't changed his plans any, just meant that he'd had to be very careful. It hadn't been easy to get the access to the horses he needed, since those horses were her life, but in the end he'd won. Not quite the way he'd imagined, but he'd won.

He wished that she'd never caught him in the barn that night, she wasn't even supposed to be on the property, but thanks to a canceled flight, she'd found him giving the horses the steroids that would guarantee him the wins he needed to really cement his reputation in the racing world. That those races came with monetary gain only heightened his pleasure.

Except that the money he'd been winning wasn't enough to pay off the debts he'd so recklessly accumulated over the time it took to get into Barbra's life. He'd been so intent on getting what he wanted, that he'd failed to take into consideration that once he started with the very expensive steroids, there would be no end to the expense.

The stress of constantly looking over his shoulder was mostly to blame for his reaction when Allison found him in the barn that night. It was really her fault, if she'd just minded her own business and let him run things as he saw fit, she'd still be alive. It hadn't helped that she'd laughed at him when he'd tried to kiss her after her mother's death. Why he'd ever thought he wanted the bitch he had no idea, but as with all other things in his life, when he was denied something he wanted it even more.

Just thinking about Allison's luscious body made his crotch stiffen, but then he remembered that she was gone, probably nothing but bones now. It had been more than a month since he'd told the boys to dump her body out here in the back part of the property, a month of lying to her friends about where she'd gone. He was actually very proud of how he'd handled the whole situation, a few carefully worded emails had satisfied all but her best friend.

Now he'd simply collect what was left of Allison, put it in a bag and sink it into the lake. Then he'd send out one more email and consider the entire episode a mistake he'd learned from. Without a body no one could prove that anything had happened to Allison, she'd simply become one of the thousands of missing adults in America.

He might eventually have to do something with her car, which was hidden in the deep forest not far from where the body had been dumped, but for now it could just sit and rust, no one ever came back here so it would be safe. When he pulled the truck over, he took a deep breath preparing himself for the task at hand. It might be very unpleasant if the scavengers hadn't done their job, it was also possible that he'd have to scour a fairly large area if they had.

When he climbed down into the ditch, he expected to see at least some sign of Allison's body, but the ditch was suspiciously empty. Assuming that the animals had pulled the body away from the road, he began to search the area but still didn't find anything, not a scrap of clothes, nothing. He was beginning to panic, there was no way the body could have completely disappeared in only a month.

After another fruitless hour of searching, his panic level was rising by the second. He'd been sure that she was dead when he'd loaded her into the back of his pickup. The boys had agreed with him, even promised that they'd checked before they disposed of the body in the ditch. But now he was questioning that assumption, he should have put a bullet in her head just to make sure.

He'd heard crazy stories about people who'd looked dead then woken up, but even if that had happened there was no way Allison could have gotten out of the woods. At the very least she would have been severely hurt, he'd smashed his gun into her head with such force that it had thrown her across the room. But if she'd survived and gotten out, then someone would have come looking for him of that he was sure.

No way would she have let an attack like that go unpunished, plus there was the little issue of the steroids. Expanding his search area, he pulled out his phone and called the boys, maybe they hadn't understood where he'd told them to dump the body. They were idiots after all, which was always the problem when you hired people like them.

Curley picked up on the first ring, "Hi boss. What's up?"

Matt cringed at his flippant tone, "I'm out here trying to clean up that little mess from last month and I can't seem to find it. You did put it where I told you to, by the old cabin at the back of the property."

"Sure boss, we did just like you said. Even managed to hide the car back in them woods too." Curley said, clearly proud of himself.

Matt got a sinking feeling in the pit of his stomach, "Are you sure she was dead when you dumped her?"

"Well, I ain't no doctor but she sure wasn't moving or nothing." Curley said, getting defensive.

"Where did you put the car?" Matt asked through clenched teeth.

"Just a little ways from where we dumped the body, if you look careful you can see a little road going back to the cabin, made it easy." Curley said, sounding surer of himself.

"Did you know that you're an idiot?" Matt said, then hung up the phone before Curley could reply.

He scrambled back up to the road, scanning the area for the road Curley had been talking about. It was hard to see, but after a few minutes Matt found it. Jumping into the truck, he followed the road until it disappeared into the forest, then got out of the truck and began to search for Allison's car. No way could a car disappear, if it was gone, he was in big trouble.

After another hour of searching, he knew that Allison hadn't been dead after all, somehow she'd survived and found the car, now she was out there somewhere with knowledge that would not only ruin him, but put him in jail for a long time. He started to panic, but then realized if she'd told anyone he'd be in jail by now. She must have run, probably hiding out somewhere afraid to show her face. That would work in his favor.

He'd find her and take care of the problem, it shouldn't be that hard, not in today's world of computers and social media. Matt had contacts all over the state, plus Allison had been on her way to Las Vegas that day so he had a place to start. Surely he could find out if she boarded that plane, and if she did then it was only a matter of time before he'd find her. Las Vegas was his playground, he had lots of people there who owed him favors.

Feeling better, he got back in the truck and started making plans to see that Allison Stevens never told anyone about the steroids or what had happened in the barn that night. If he was really lucky this might just work in his favor and he'd get to fulfill that fantasy he had of dominating her before he killed her. This job was for him alone, no way was he going to trust those idiots he'd hired this time.

*****

Allison woke up early the next morning with Nate's strong chest pressed up against her back and his hand on her breast. She knew she should get out of bed and see Garrett and Sabrina off on their honeymoon. They'd left the wedding so early last night that she'd barely said two words to them and felt guilty. She was sure they would not only understand, but applaud her decision to move on with her life.

She tried to slide out of bed, but Nate's arm clamped down more tightly when she moved. "Where do you think you're going?" He asked, his voice husky with sleep.

"I need to talk to Garrett and Sabrina before they leave." She said, turning to face him.

"What time is it?" He asked, throwing his leg over hers, pinning her in the bed.

"The sun's just coming up so it must be close to seven." She said, wiggling to try and get out of his grip.

"Then we have plenty of time before the family descends on the house." He said, nuzzling her neck.

"Nate, stop that right now. I need to shower before breakfast and so do you, stop messing around." She said, pushing against his chest, but feeling her desire beginning to build.

"Hmm, I'm not messing around yet." He said, rolling her onto her back. "But that's a really good idea."

Somehow he'd managed to position himself between her legs, making her heart beat race. He was clearly aroused, his erection just inches from entering her. With a sigh, she said, "Well, we might have a few minutes." Then took him in her hands and guided him inside her.

More than an hour later, they finally emerged from her room. Nate dashed down the hall dressed only in a towel to get dressed, making her laugh. Everyone was gathered in the kitchen, most saying their goodbyes since Garrett and Sabrina were off on a three week honeymoon. The kids were going to stay with Daphne and Allison had agreed to keep an eye on the house and barns while they were gone.

Sabrina spotted her first and pulled her into the sun room. "I'm glad to see you this morning. You left early last night and I was worried, but Garret said you left with Nate."

"I'm sorry about that, but the wedding brought on some difficult memories, I stayed as long as I could." Allison said, feeling guilty.

"Are you okay today?" Sabrina asked, the concern clear on her face.

"Actually, I'm really fine. Nate's been wonderful, helping me work through everything." She said, finding it impossible to suppress the huge grin that spread across her face.

Sabrina knew that look only too well, "I think you're in good hands. Has he told you if he plans to stay?"

"No, but he hasn't talked about leaving either. I hope that's okay." Allison said, thinking if Nate left she'd go with him, then realizing how selfish that was, changed her mind.

"He's welcome to stay as long as he wants, but I'm sure we'll get to talk to him before we leave. Most of the guests left early this morning to make flights out of Denver." Sabrina said, enjoying the look of pleasure that appeared on Allison's face.

"Good, he can help me with the horses." Allison said, thinking of all the other things he might help her with.

"He's a good man, I'm happy for you."

Allison blushed to think that their relationship was so obvious, but then realized who she was talking to. "I hope I haven't rushed into something that will hurt me in the end."

"Trust your instincts, I see how Nate looks at you and how you look at him. I've been there before, I was never much of a believer in fate, but something put Garrett in my life and I've been thankful ever since."

"Thanks Sabrina, I don't know what I would have done if you all hadn't taken me in." Allison said, hugging her. "Go have fun on your honeymoon. I'll take care of everything here."

"I know you will. Now let's go get you some breakfast and find that man of yours." Sabrina said, taking her hand.

Allison liked the sound of that, Nate was her man, a man any woman would love to have. He was leaning up against the counter when she walked into the kitchen with Sabrina, deep in conversation with Garrett. When he saw her, he poured her a cup of coffee and crossed the room to hand it to her. If that wasn't message enough, he then put his arm around her possessively.

"Garrett had just invited me to stay and help you with the ranch while they're gone." Nate said, pulling her a little closer.

"I don't really want you here by yourself Allison. I hope that's okay." Garrett said.

"Of course. Thank you. I'd like him to stay."

"Well, now we've settled that, we need to get moving." Garrett said, heading for the entry way where he'd left their luggage. "If you need anything just call Daphne, the rest of the guests will be gone by tonight and Esmerelda will be here to clean the house tomorrow."

Nate and Allison walked them out to the car, "Have fun and don't worry, everything here will be just fine."

When they got back in the house, they looked at each other and smiled. For all intents and purposes they had the house to themselves for the next three weeks. Nate was just considering the chances of getting Allison back up to her bedroom, but she had other plans.

"Are you ready to learn how to clean a stall?" She asked, a grin on her face.

"Well, I should really check my email and see if there's any new information." He said, grinning back at her.

"Sounds like a good excuse to me." She said, "But don't think you're getting out of it next time."

Nate did manage to get out of cleaning stalls, Allison didn't really mind the work and it kept her occupied. With no riders coming to the ranch while Sabrina was gone, there wasn't much else for her to do. Nate spent most of his time in the library on his computer, she knew he wasn't working on her case all that time, because he kept her updated on any new information that came in.

There hadn't been any new information for days, but Allison had come to terms with her situation and most of her anxiety had evaporated when she'd made the decision. It also helped that she slept safe in Nate's arms each night, after they'd made love. He had a way of calming her fears while forcing her to face them. But as the days passed, she decided that it was time she found out more about him. It seemed to her that he was being very careful about revealing his past.

She'd been so caught up in her own problems, she hadn't given his life away from the ranch much thought. Other than the fact that he'd been a detective for twenty years, came from Kentucky, and had lost both of his parents, she knew very little about him. She wondered how such a great guy had remained single all these years.

After Garrett and Sabrina had been gone for a week, Allison found herself with an afternoon completely free which was not a good thing. Since the therapy rides had been canceled, there was little to keep her occupied once the horses were cared for. Sabrina had said that she didn't need to worry about exercising them, but with nothing else to do she'd decided that a ride would be just the thing to pass the afternoon.

Even better, she'd decided to take Nate with her, she had a sneaking suspicion that he couldn't ride and it was time to remedy that situation. She found him in the library, where he spent most of his time on his computer. Walking into the room, she knocked on the door jam, then walked over to the desk wondering what it was he'd been working on for the last two days.

"What are you up to in here?" She asked coming over to stand beside him.

He swiveled around in his chair to face her, then pulled her onto his lap. "Thinking about you instead of working." He said, kissing her.

"Hmm, that's nice to hear. I've been thinking about you too. How about going for a ride with me?" She asked, grinning at him.

"Well, tell me more about what you had in mind. There are several different rides I'd like to take you on." He said, reaching up her shirt and unhooking her bra.

Allison was instantly on her feet, "Not that kind of ride." She said, laughing as she hooked her bra again. "I was thinking more about riding a horse. You've been cooped up in here all week, let's go get some fresh air."

"I couldn't talk you into a nice warm car ride?" He countered.

"Stop being a baby and go find your coat, it's actually pretty warm out there today. Come on, up you go." She said, pulling him out of his chair.

"I really should finish what I was working on." He said, looking back at the computer.

"You never did tell me what you were working on." She said, handing him his coat. "Is it a case? I thought you were on leave."

He took her hand as they walked to the barn, "It's kind of embarrassing, but I guess I should tell you about my plans." He said, giving her hand a squeeze. "But first you're going to have to give me a riding lesson."

They spent the next half an hour saddling their horses, Nate did his best but it was clear that horses were not his thing. She would have sworn that the horse she'd chosen for him had taken an instant dislike to him, doing everything possible to keep him from getting the saddle on her including holding her breath when he tried to cinch it down.

"If you don't make her blow that lung full of air out before you tighten the cinch, you're going to end up on the ground." Allison laughed, wondering how long the horse could hold her breath.

"I'm trying, but I have no idea how to make a horse breathe?" Nate said, clearly getting frustrated.

"Walk around in front of her and blow in her nose." Allison suggested.

It worked but Nate ended up with a shirt full of horse snot, still he quickly got the saddle tightened. "Thanks for the advice." He said, shooting her a dirty look.

Allison was trying not to laugh, but finally couldn't help herself. "I'm sorry, I didn't think she'd do that. I never have any problem getting the saddle on her, obviously she's smart to that trick."

"Well, I guess it was worth it to see you laughing, but I'm going to need a shower after this." He said, following her as she led the horses out of the barn.

"I can help with that." She said, shooting him a big smile. "It's the least I can do since it's my fault."

"That makes it worth it." He said, coming up next to her at the hitching rail. "I just hope riding her will be easier than saddling her was."

Nate got his wish, it seemed that he'd won a battle with the horse, who behaved herself after that. By the time they'd reached the far pasture, he'd found his seat and was actually enjoying himself. Allison seemed perfectly at home on the back of a horse, as if it was second nature for her, he was a little bit jealous that there was an entire part of her life that he wasn't a part of but that could be fixed easily enough. He'd never been a fan of horses, but riding with Allison on a beautiful sunny day was quickly making him reconsider that.

## Chapter 6

Allison hadn't forgotten that he'd promised to tell her what he'd been doing all day. "So you said you'd tell me what you've been working on in the library." She said, trying to sound nonchalant when in truth she was extremely curious about his life.

"It's a little bit embarrassing but I've been taking on line classes to get my degree in architecture." He said, not meeting her eyes.

"What's embarrassing about that? Sounds like a great thing to me."

He finally met her eyes, which were shining in the winter sun, making him wish they were cuddled up on their favorite couch in the sunroom. "I'm over forty, it's a little late to be making a career change. I just feel silly when I say I'm going to college."

"Nate, lots of people change their career at some point during their lives. Is this something you've always wanted to do?"

He shook his head yes, then said, "Ever since I was a kid. The other boys wanted to play baseball and video games, I wanted to explore old buildings and build Lego towns." He said, smiling at the memory.

"What happened?"

"My dad got sick just as I graduated from high school and there was no way I could leave home to go away to college. I did a couple of years at the local community college, then joined the police force. Don't get me wrong, I've enjoyed my job and actually seem to have a talent for it, but I really want to design buildings." He said, shrugging his shoulders.

"Then you should. What kind of buildings?" She asked, worried that she would lose him to this passion she'd known nothing about. It seemed to her that architects always worked in big cities. Even as little as she knew about herself, she knew that city living was definitely not for her.

"Actually, I don't want to design new buildings, I want to restore old ones. Did you see the old buildings down town, those are a restoration dream. I'd love to get my hands on one of them. There's one that is just screaming for someone to come in and shore it up. It would make a great restaurant or even a bar, I can see the whole thing in my mind."

Allison was quiet as they made their way back to the barn, "That's not what I expected at all, but I think it's great. How much longer do you have before you get your degree?"

"I'm almost done. One more class then I have to pass the state boards." He said, then added. "It's taken me five years, but it was my dad's last request before he died. He'd always felt guilty that I wasn't able to pursue my dreams. In fact, thanks to him and some wise investments he made before he died, I have a nice nest egg."

Allison was getting more worried by the second, Nate obviously had big plans for the rest of his life, and she had no idea how she fit into those plans. "So where is all this going to happen, do you have specific plans?" She asked, trying not to sound like she asked for an invitation to join him.

"Honestly, I hadn't thought that far in advance, but I can't seem to get my mind off the building in town. I wonder who owns it, I'd like to find out how much they want for it."

"I can tell you who owns that property easily." She said, surprised that he didn't know.

"Really, how?"

"I thought you knew that the Terrell's own the entire town."

"The entire town? But what about all the people that live there?"

"They all have some form of a long term lease. There are a few privately owned properties, but nothing in town."

Nate considered this for a few minutes, "I had no idea. This makes things even more complicated that I'd first thought."

"The Terrell's are worth billions, you should ask Jonathan about the family history some time. They've owned all this land for generations, not only the ski resort but thousands of acres of untamed forest."

Nate suddenly realized that he might have made a mistake not telling his brothers who he was from the beginning. It had made sense when he thought the ranch was the only wealth they had, but now realizing the true scope of their wealth made him even more nervous that they would think he was only out for a cut.

"What do you mean, it only makes things more complicated?" Allison asked, beginning to realize that there was a lot more to this man than she'd discovered.

"Nothing, I was just thinking out loud." Nate said, hoping that she'd let the subject drop. He knew he had to tell her the truth soon, but for some reason he didn't feel like right now was the right time. She too might be suspicious of his motivation, or angry that he hadn't told her before now. Suddenly he was feeling foolish that he'd backed himself into a corner.

When they got back to the house, Nate made a bee line for the shower, dragging Allison with him. They'd been quiet since he'd refused to answer her question and he could understand why. Suddenly she'd discovered that there was more to him then just her savior, she'd come to depend on him and he'd suddenly told her about a part of his life that didn't include her.

He'd been fooling himself to think that they'd just slip into this relationship without some of his secrets coming to light, but she had no idea how big of a secret he was carrying around with him. He'd come here to discover his roots, and instead fallen head over heels for Allison, which had distracted him from his original purpose. It was time to make a visit to Jonathan, his father, he'd have to do something one way or another when Garrett and Sabrina got back.

Either he needed to share his secret or take Allison and leave. One thing he knew for certain, he wasn't leaving here without her. After their shower, he suggested a trip to visit Jonathan and Cinthia. Allison readily agreed since she loved the couple like they were her parents, but was surprised that Nate had suggested it. In all the time they'd been here it had seemed like he had been avoiding them, now he was suggesting a visit.

She was almost sorry she'd asked about what he'd been doing on the computer, ever since then things had been off balance. Finding out more about him had been her goal, but maybe she should have left well enough alone. Of course she knew that there was no way they could live the rest of their lives in the bubble they found themselves in right now, still it would have been nice if it had lasted a little longer.

When they got to Jonathan and Cinthia's house the couple was glad to see them. "It's been too quiet around here since Garrett and Sabrina have been gone. It seems like all the kids disappeared at once." Cinthia said, leading them into the kitchen where she'd have some wonderful treat for them.

"It has been quiet. I thought it would be nice, but I'm afraid I miss all the commotion." Allison said, helping Cinthia get everyone coffee.

"We moved out here by ourselves thinking the same thing, but I find myself over there as much as here."

"But you get to come home to your own quiet house at night. It's a perfect situation."

"Yes, it is and I'm very lucky, all my daughter in laws are wonderful women who are perfect for my sons." Cinthia said smiling.

The men had long since taken their coffee out to the barn, a typical move for the Terrell men, Allison though when she realized they were gone. "Well, they managed to sneak off pretty quick."

"Men, you know how they are." Cinthia said, wondering herself what they were talking about.

*****

Jonathan knew this visit was significant, Nate had been avoiding him any time they were together, he understood why, but was anxious to move past this awkward phase. He also wanted Nate to tell his other sons who he was, it was serving no purpose keeping them in the dark. Hopefully, that was what this visit was about.

"How's everything going over at the ranch? Are you keeping yourselves occupied over there?" Jonathan asked, leading Nate into the barn, where it was warm. Although the day had been warm, once the sun set the temperature dropped dramatically. It had taken him by surprise the first time, but since then he'd learned to always have his coat with him.

"We're fine, Allison has made the decision to move on with her life, I'm still trying to figure out who she is, but for now she's living for the future instead of trying to remember the past. That's part of the reason I'm here. I think I've made a mistake not telling everyone who I really am." He said, looking at the man who he was just beginning to think of as his father.

"Does this mean that you're ready to tell them?"

"I think I must, I need to tell Allison as well and if I tell her I have to tell them. Suddenly, I have all these choices to make, life used to be so simple. Sometimes I think it might be easier to just go back home and forget about this whole thing. It's almost like a dream." Nate said, all the frustration he'd been blocking for the last few weeks suddenly coming to the surface.

"Son, you've been though a lot in the last few months, heck I'd say you've been through a lot in the last few years. You want my advice, tell everyone who you are and why you're here as soon as you can, that will be one less thing weighing on your mind." Jonathan said, putting his hand on Nate's shoulder, pleased when Nate let it rest there.

"That might fix the problems with the family, but I'm scared I've made a mistake getting involved with Allison.

There could be real disaster in our future if it turns out that she'd married or something." Nate said, dejectedly.

"What does your gut tell you?"

"That if there was someone out there who cared about her they would have been looking for her everywhere. If she was mine I would be, but it's been weeks and no one has reported her missing. This isn't television, things like that don't happen in real life. I've been going over it and over it in my mind and I honestly believe she's alone." Nate said, his conviction getting stronger when he said it out loud.

"I have to agree with you. My next question is simple. How do you feel about her?"

Nate thought about that for a long time, then finally said, "She's sexy and smart, caring and compassionate, and everything I ever wanted in a woman." He said, turning to look at Jonathan. "I think I'm falling in love with her."

"Then you have to ask yourself if it matters that you know nothing about her past, nor does she. Someday those things may come back to her, but right now you're going to have to make a blind leap of faith that things will work out."

"But what if they don't? I don't know if I can stand the heartbreak."

"Well, if that happens, know that we'll all be here to help you pick up the pieces." Jonathan said, "We're your family now and that's what family does. Now we better get back in the house, I'd like you to get to know Cinthia. She's a wonderful woman, I hope someday you two can be close."

They were almost to the door when Jonathan suddenly stopped. "I almost forgot, I want you to take these." He said, placing two rings in Nate's hand.

Nate picked up the larger of the two, it was obviously a man's ring, made of heavy gold it had a family crest on it in tiny little diamonds. He looked up from the ring in his fingers to Jonathan, wondering what the ring meant.

"I gave all my boys one of those rings when they turned 21, I'm sorry yours is a bit late, but I still wanted you to have one. That's our family crest, your grandfather several generations back thought that it would elevate the family, it's a silly custom but it's ours."

Nate was speechless, he'd never been a part of a family like the Terrell's but he was quickly beginning to like the feeling. "And the other ring?" He asked, his voice cracking with emotion.

"That's for your bride. Every Terrell woman wears a piece of the family jewelry when she marries into the clan. I have a feeling you might be needing that in a few months, but just because you have it don't get carried away. Give yourselves time, don't rush into anything, neither of you needs to go anywhere."

Nate couldn't help himself, he wrapped his arms around Jonathan, and hugged him. Jonathan was surprised at first, but hugged him back, smiling like he'd just won the lottery. Once they had their emotions under control, they headed back to the house, Nate feeling like a giant weight had been lifted off his shoulders, sure that things would work themselves out in the end.

Cinthia and Allison were having a conversation of their own since the men had disappeared. "Dear, I don't want to pry, but I can't help but notice that something has changed.

Have you remembered anything new?" Cinthia asked, not sure what was different about Allison.

"No, nothing since the wedding, but I've decided to stop trying so hard to figure out who I am and concentrate on building a new life." Allison said, hoping that Cinthia would think this was progress.

"I think that's an excellent idea." She said, patting Allison's hand. "Does Nate have anything to do with this?"

"He might." She said, smiling. "As much as it hurts me to admit it, there's no one out there looking for me and Nate's here."

"He seems like a nice young man, just promise me you'll take your time. Don't rush into anything."

"I may have already done that." Allison said, blushing.

"I don't mean sex, I mean don't make promises to one another that you may not be able to keep. Love is fun and exciting at first, but if you don't do the work, it won't last. You and Nate have some other problems to deal with as well."

Cinthia said, then must have realized she'd said too much because she got up and began clearing the table.

"I know my memories are an issue, but you make it sound like there are other issues as well. Why do I feel like I'm missing something?"

Cinthia was relieved that the men came back into the kitchen just then, she'd been searching for a way to avoid answering Allison's question. It wasn't her place to tell Allison who Nate really was, she wished that the whole situation would go away. She had to admit that his presence was disturbing for her, she'd long ago forgiven Jonathan for the affair, but seeing the product of that affair had been harder than she'd expected.

But she was a Terrell through and through, she'd learn to accept Nate as one of their own, in time she'd probably be glad he'd come into their lives, but for now she needed time to get used to the idea. It wasn't easy to accept that your husband's oldest son wasn't yours as well. She hoped that Jonathan's belief that the boys would accept him with open arms was true, because if it wasn't they were in for a rough time.

*****

They were both quiet on the ride home, each lost in their own thought. Nate was trying to figure out how to tell Allison about his real reason for being in Colorado. Allison worrying about what it was she was missing, everyone seemed to have some secret they were keeping about Nate, she tried to imagine what could be so important that he was keeping it secret, hopefully it wasn't a wife somewhere.

She'd never flat out asked him if he was involved or married, but he'd said that he was alone so that didn't make sense. Finally she gave up, she'd just have to keep digging into his life, whether he liked it or not. As much as she liked Nate, she wasn't going to find herself in love with a man who couldn't or wouldn't return that love.

Nate could sense Allison's distress and knew he'd have to tell her tonight, it wasn't fair to put her in this position and he owed her the honesty. He was worried about how she would take the news, but once he'd told her, they could move forward with their lives together, everything would be out in the open. It would feel good to tell her, it had been bothering him since they'd spent the night together, but she'd been in no shape that night to hear his confession, it would have only confused the situation.

As soon as they walked in the door, Nate went to his bedroom and got the photo album his mom had given him and left it in the sunroom, once dinner was over, he'd tell her. They were quiet at dinner, both conscious that something had changed. As soon as dinner was over, Nate convinced Allison to leave the dishes and join him in the sunroom.

Allison was suddenly very nervous, she knew Nate was about to tell her what he'd been avoiding all day. It could mean the end of their relationship, then she'd be alone again.

"Sit down, I want to show you something. I should have told you this a long time ago, but there just wasn't a good time. I hope you'll understand." He said, pulling her down onto the couch with him.

He put the photo album in her lap, then opened it to the first page. Allison looked at him mystified, this wasn't what she'd expected. But as she looked at the picture she realized that she recognized two of the people in the old back and white photo. "That's Jonathan and Cinthia." She said.

"Yes, and those are my parents with them, they were friends in college. Evidently the two couples were inseparable, hung out together all the time." He said, turning the pages.

Allison saw wedding photos of the couples, then the next pages were a series of photos of the Terrell family. "So they must have stayed in touch all these years." She said, still unable to see where this was going.

"No, I'm afraid they had a falling out. It all started with Jonathan and Cinthia fighting about her finishing college before they got married, but the end result was that my mother and Jonathan had a short affair." He said, taking a deep breath, it was still hard to say that his mother had slept with another man besides his father. A boy wasn't supposed to think of his mother as a sexual person, it just wasn't done.

"Oh, that's...." Allison didn't know what to say.

Nate took another deep breath, "My mother and Jonathan came to their senses pretty quickly and the couples got back together, each ended up married shortly after that."

"So there was a happy ending." Allison said, relieved but still not sure why he was telling her all this.

"Well, yeah I guess, except that my mother was already pregnant with me before they got married."

# Chapter 7

Allison thought about this for a minute then she understood. "Jonathan is your father. Does he know?" She asked, understanding all the implications of what he'd just told her. "Do the boys know?"

"Jonathan and Cinthia do, they've known for a long time even though my mother never told them. He said he wasn't completely sure until he saw me. I haven't told anyone else but you." He said, waiting for her to get angry, which the other women he'd dated would have done.

"Oh, Nate. I don't know if that's awful or wonderful. On the one hand, you're not who you always thought you were, but on the other hand now you have a whole new family."

"I was angry at first, but I've come to the conclusion that it's a wonderful thing. The Terrell's are a wonderful family, a family anyone would be proud to be a part of, but they may not be as thrilled with me as I am with them." He said, breathing a sigh of relief that Allison wasn't mad.

"I haven't known them for that long but they seem like reasonable men, they may be upset at first, but in the end they'll accept you, I just know it." She said, setting the photo album on the coffee table and sliding closer to him.

"You're not mad that I didn't tell you sooner?" He asked, putting his arm around her.

"No, I understand. You wanted to check out the situation before you told them, I would have done the same. Are you ready to tell them now?" She asked, thinking that her future was suddenly tied up in how the Terrell brothers took this news.

"Yes, and I wish I'd told them sooner. I'm worried that they'll think I'm only here to lay some kind of claim on all this." He said, gesturing around the room.

"They don't seem like the kind of people who would think that, besides you told me yourself that you have money of your own, I'm sure it's nothing like their money but still."

"I know you're probably right, but now that I've made the decision to tell them, I just want to get it over with." He said, getting up and pacing the room. "It's like waiting to tell your parents that you've done something wrong."

Allison got up from the couch and went to Nate where he was looking out the window. "I think it might be my turn to help you get your mind off your problems. Things will work out, you'll see." She said, wrapping her arms around his solid back.

"Really, what did you have in mind?" He asked, turning in her arms.

"Did you lock the door and set the alarm?" She asked, unbuttoning his shirt.

"Yes." He said, sucking in a breath when she ran her hands down his chest to the buckle of his pants then back up his chest.

She slid the shirt off his shoulders, then stood on her toes to kiss him, hands still on his chest. Nate pulled her shirt over her head then tried to pull her to him, but she pushed him back. Instead, she found the sensitive spot at the base of his ear and teased it with her tongue. She could feel Nate stiffen, then relax with a growl in his throat.

Teasing and kissing, she moved down his neck and across his chest, his hands found their way to her hair and tangled there. She unbuttoned his pants and freed his erection stroking it with her hand until Nate threw his head back in pleasure. Sinking to her knees, she unlaced his boots and removed them, then looking up at him, she pulled his pants down and waited while he stepped out of them.

On her knees in front of him, she looked up at him while taking his throbbing penis in her hand. There was a gleaming drop of pre-cum on the tip, darting her tongue out she licked it off, making Nate stagger a little with the intensity of the feeling. Her tongue was hot, making him want to feel all of her mouth on him.

Still stroking him, she licked her lips then slid her mouth over his hard length, taking as much of him as she could into her mouth. Allison felt the power of her sexuality when she saw the look of pleasure that appeared on Nate's face. She could feel the wetness soaking her panties, but wasn't ready to relinquish her control.

Nate's entire body was on fire as Allison took him into her mouth and sucked greedily, seeing her brown eyes watching him as she did only intensified the pleasure. But all too soon, his body took over and he began to thrust his hips as she sucked on him. His fingers tangled in her silky hair, bringing her mouth closer, allowing him to go deeper, until he felt the back of her throat with the tip of his cock.

After only a few thrusts he knew that he would cum right in her mouth if he didn't slow things down, pulling her to her feet he, found her mouth in a searing kiss that left them both breathless. He unhooked her bra and found a stiff peak with his mouth, making Allison groan with pleasure.

Switching to the other breast, his hands gripping her butt, he slid one knee between her legs, pushing her legs open. One hand slid around and rubbed her through her pants, her wetness soaking through. Then sinking to his knees, he removed her shoes and slid her pants off. Her body was alive with desire, anticipation making her stomach tighten as his hand slid up her legs to the juncture of her thighs. He slid his hand between her legs, causing her to part them slightly again.

Her hands on his shoulders, she was trembling as he slid his fingers between her folds and stroked her clit. Eyes locked on hers, he rubbed her clit until she dug her nails into his back, moaning his name. Allison was on the brink of an orgasm, but before she could crest the wave, Nate stood up and picked her up and placed her on the couch.

Kneeling between her legs, he spread them and slid his finger inside her, his eyes never leaving hers. Allison was assaulted by not only the feeling of his finger inside her, but the look in his eyes as he bought her pleasure. As the waves of pleasure flooded her body, she gripped his shoulders sure that she couldn't take any more. But Nate lowered his mouth and with his finger still insider her, ran his tongue over her swollen clit.

Her orgasm was immediate, suffusing her with a pleasure so intense, she cried out his name. As the waves of pleasure began to subside, she felt an intense need to feel him inside her. "Nate, I need you inside me. I want to feel you filling me up." She begged.

Allison begging him released a new wave of desire in him, surpassing anything he'd ever felt before. Coming up off his knees, Nate grabbed Allison and spun her around on the couch, positioning her so that her arms were resting on the back. Then he spread her legs, grabbed her hips and buried himself inside her.

It happened so fast that Allison hardly had time to breathe before he was deep inside her, filling her like she'd wanted, deep and hard. Nate ground his hips against Allison before pulling out of her and filling her again, but this time he began to thrust in and out of her, his hand holding her hips. Allison's body responded by clenching down around his swollen penis.

Allison was beyond thought, the pressure building to a hard center deep inside her. Every nerve ending in her body was aware of Nate, his hard muscles, the way he smelled, even the sound of his grunts as he took what he wanted from her. Nate knew that he couldn't hold off much longer but wanted to feel Allison cum with him so he reached around and found her clit, stroking it until he felt her muscles beginning to tremble with pleasure.

Allison's orgasm crested in a glorious rush, the feeling of Nate's fingers stroking her making it go on and on, his hips grinding into hers bringing an even deeper pleasure washing over her in almost gentle waves. It was an orgasm like she'd never experienced before, deeper and more satisfying than she'd ever imagined one could be.

Nate felt Allison's body respond to his fingers, her muscles contracting around him, but it felt deeper this time, tumbling him over the edge in a soul shattering orgasm that left him breathless and spent. Muscles trembling, he pulled Allison down onto the couch and snuggled up to her back, arms wrapped around her, still breathing hard from the force of his orgasm.

It was a long time before either of them spoke, both floating in a river of satisfaction, the web of pleasure still woven tightly around them. Allison was sure she'd never felt such intense emotion with anyone else, memories or not, she knew what she and Nate shared was special. Nate more content than he'd ever been in his life, trying to figure out how to keep this woman in his life forever.

"That was the best distraction I've ever had." He said, kissing the back of her neck.

"I'll definitely have to use those distraction techniques again." She said, laughing.

"Allison, thank you." He said, turning serious.

She turned in his arms to look at him, "For what?" She asked, perplexed.

"For understanding why I didn't tell you and everyone else the truth to begin with." He said, kissing her forehead.

Allison looked at him, thinking about how hard it must have been to hear his mother's story only weeks before her death. "It makes sense to me that you'd want to meet them before you told them who you were, Jonathan already knew so it wasn't like it was a complete secret. As for not telling me, I understand that as well, you were probably still trying to adjust to the idea yourself."

"When I got here I'd only known they existed for a few weeks, I couldn't just knock on the door and announce that I was the long lost son, home at last. The thing that surprises me is that they didn't figure it out right away. Even I can see the resemblance between the four of us, Cinthia spotted it right away."

"People don't always see what's right in front of their faces, it's not like they were expecting a brother they never knew they had to show up on their door step. Plus they were all distracted by the wedding, it's probably a good idea that you tell them when Garrett and Sabrina get home."

"That's what I was thinking, at some point they're going to wonder what I'm doing here and start asking questions."

"They'll be home in a week, you can tell them then. In the meantime, let's go to bed. I might just have another distraction for you." She said, pulling him to his feet.

"Hmm, I like the sound of that." He said, wrapping his arm around her waist as they mounted the stairs to her room. "I might need a lot of distracting next week." He added, his hand sinking lower.

*****

Garrett and Sabrina arrived home amidst much fanfare and celebration. Leslie and Sebastian had arrived the day before from their own vacation, while Elizabeth and Donovan, the baby in tow had been closing up their house in the city. After much persuasion from Elizabeth, Donovan had decided to move his office to Pleasant Valley so they could live at the ranch full time.

Terrell Industries would still have an office in the city, but all his personal staff was moving with him. Allison had been enjoying watching the play between the two, Elizabeth wanted him to build her a new cabin on the property, but he though the one they had was fine. As of the wedding, no agreement had been reached and she was curious to find out who'd come out the winner. Her money was on Elizabeth, but she didn't know Donovan all that well.

It was a shock to realize that she'd become a part of these people lives so quickly, but she was also thankful for the opportunity. It scared her that Nate's announcement was going to shatter that closeness, and she really hoped she wouldn't have to choose between the two. Nate hadn't told her how he planned to tell them, he probably didn't have a plan. It would be impossible with this group to plan it.

Allison was nervous though dinner, sensing the same in Nate, but trying to remain calm for his sake. This was about him, not her, she needed to be supportive instead of worrying about her own fears. After desert, Nate cleared his throat and she though he was going to tell everyone while they were still seated at the dining room table, but instead he asked Garrett for a private word.

There was a brief silence around the table, but Jonathan quickly filled it, asking Leslie about their trip to Hawaii. Conversation resumed and soon they all took their coffee to the living room, Allison was distracted by what might be happening in the other room, until Elizabeth sat down next to her, and she allowed herself to be distracted.

When Garrett heard Nate asking him for a private meeting, he knew what was coming. The minute Nate had walked in the door, he'd seen the resemblance. It hadn't taken Donovan long to piece the story together, a few internet searches and some phone calls had given him all the information he'd needed. While he'd accepted the fact that Nate existed, he wanted to hear for himself what the man had to say. Nate seemed like an honest and upstanding man, but appearances could be deceiving.

Nate followed Garrett back to the library, the most logical place for them to a talk, which Nate had been counting on. Earlier he'd put the photo album on one of the shelves, anticipating this meeting and how he'd introduce the subject. Picking up the album he handed it to Garrett, then indicated that he should look at it. Garrett paged though the album, then closed it.

"Is there some significance to this?" He asked, in his gruffest voice. "Where did you get this?"

"My mother gave it to me right before she died. There's no easy way to say this, but she kept that album because Jonathan is my father. She told me that they had an affair right before she married my dad, she didn't know she was pregnant, but when I was born she was sure." Nate said, rushing the words he'd so carefully rehearsed.

"So, let me get this straight, you're my half-brother? The product of my father and another woman while he was dating my mother?" Garrett said, enjoying seeing Nate's face go pale at his words.

"Well, she said that they'd broken up, but the affair made them both realize what they were missing and they ended it." Nate said, embarrassed for all of them.

"As much as I'd like to call you a liar, this does make sense of several hushed conversations between my parents. But, what is it you want from us? I suppose you think you're entitled to a share of the family fortune." Garrett said coldly.

"I don't care about the money, I am fine on my own. Honestly, I didn't even know if I'd make contact with you when I drove out here. I just got in the car and drove, my mom had just been buried and I felt unconnected to my life."

"But here you are. Why didn't you tell us from the very beginning?" Garrett was struggling to keep up the pretense, but just managed.

"Would you have? I wanted to see what you all were like. Pictures don't begin to tell the story. I guess it's in my nature to be suspicious." Nate said, shrugging.

"And now you've decided that we're good enough for you?" Garrett said, still suppressing a smile.

"It's not like that, I would have told you sooner, but with Allison and her problems I just pushed it aside. Then the wedding, and you've been gone for three weeks." Nate had the terrible feeling that this wasn't going to go his way when all of the sudden Garrett burst out laughing.

"I'm sorry Nate, consider that the first of many brotherly pranks you're going to have to endure. We've know who you were almost since that first day. You didn't think we'd notice that you look like a Terrell, not to mention the fact that people in town kept saying they'd seen me in town when I wasn't."

"So you've known all this time?" Nate said, letting out his breath in a whoosh of relief.

"Did you really think I'd leave you here with my home and Allison if I hadn't checked you out? From everything I can see, you're a good man, who dedicated his life to his job and his family. Terrell traits if I've ever seen them."

"I wondered, you seemed so willing to let me just move into your lives. It just didn't make sense to me." Nate said, relaxing for the first time in weeks.

"We're pretty protective of the one's we love around here. I wasn't about to let you anywhere near the family until I investigated. I'm sure you can understand that." Garrett said, rising to his feet.

"I would have done the same thing. I guess I'd better go face everyone else. Does everyone know?" Nate asked, following Garrett to the door.

"Have you ever tried to keep a secret from a woman? I would have told Sabrina eventually, but she figured it out almost as soon as I did. I think she might have tricked mom into telling her something." Garrett said, laughing. "Nothing gets past her. Are you ready to face the family, brother?"

"As ready as I'll ever be." Nate said, following Garrett down the hall.

When they walked into the room, everyone fell silent, all eyes turned to them. Jonathan got up and went to stand behind Garrett and Nate, lending his silent support. Nate sucked in a deep breath, but couldn't seem to find any words.

Garrett, deciding that he'd put Nate through enough already, spoke up instead. "Nate's finally decided that we're good enough to be his family."

Everyone gasped, then started laughing. Donovan and Sebastian got to their feet and shook his hand. "It's about time. What took you so long?" Sebastian said, thumping him on the back.

"I just wasn't sure how you all would react to the news. It's kind of hard to suddenly realize you're not who you thought you were, and frankly you all are a lot to take in."

"Well, you're stuck with us now." Donovan said, then added, "And we have a lot of time to make up for."

The first thing Garrett did was move Nate out to one of the cabins on the property, a grown man shouldn't be living with his brother he'd decided. He also offered to take Nate to Denver to arrange for his inclusion in the Terrell Family Trust, but Nate was in no hurry. Money wasn't an issue, although he'd have to go back to Kentucky at some point to take care of selling both his house and his parents.

"Are you sure? You'll be cutting all your ties out there? Why not keep the property and rent it out?" Garrett had asked, when Nate had told him of his plans.

"Well, I wanted to talk to you about that. I saw a property in town that I'd like to lease and restore, I need the capital to take on the project. I've been studying the town and I think there might be room for another restaurant."

"You know, you won't have to lease it, it belongs to the family, if you want to renovate that building, put together a plan and we'll arrange a meeting with the board of directors. If they approve it, you won't need to invest your own money." Garrett said, shaking his head, it seemed his brother couldn't get it through his head, that he was now a full-fledged member of the family.

"But....." Nate started to protest.

"You want to be a restoration architect, then go for it. We own property all over the state, some of it is just begging for someone to love it again." Garrett said, shrugging his shoulders. "Anything you do will only increase its value."

Nate couldn't believe his ears, plans already forming in his mind. "First I have to pass my state boards, but I'd love to take a look at that property down town, I can start making plans now."

## Chapter 8

Allison was happy to see Nate bonding with his brothers and making plans for the future, plans that included her. But she was hesitant when he asked her to move to the cabin with him. "I don't know Nate, think about it. If we'd met some other way would you be asking me to move in this fast?"

Nate had to think about that for a minute, "I'm not sure, maybe. I just thought it made sense, we're together every night anyway." He said, trying not to get upset. Then realized that this is what everyone had been warning him about, he was rushing things, forgetting that Allison was still dealing with her loss of memory.

"And I'm not saying that it will be any different once you move out of the house, in face I'm glad we'll have some privacy. But, I have so little that's mine." Allison said, hoping he'd understand.

"The cabin would be ours, but I think I understand." Nate said, thinking about her words some more. "You know that we'll get to the bottom of this eventually, either I'll figure it out or you'll remember, but I'll be patient."

"Thank you, now let's get you moved into your new cabin. Have you seen it yet?" She said, relieved that they'd made it through their first disagreement.

Nate was disappointed that Allison didn't want to move in with him, but realized that it was the best decision, what he also realized was that their relationship wasn't going to be able to move any further until Allison regained her memory. It made finding out her identity suddenly the most important thing in his life. A trip home might be a good idea, he was still convinced that she was from Kentucky, after all, the flight she'd been on had come out of Louisville.

Whether or not he decided to sell the property back in Kentucky, he still needed to go back and pack up both places which could take several weeks. He hated to leave Allison, but he'd already been gone for months and doubted that he'd ever return, so leaving the houses sitting empty for any longer was just asking for some kind of disaster. He'd decide when he got back there whether he'd keep the properties or sell them.

He'd have to deal with his job as well, his plans had been to stay on the force until he'd passed his board, but he'd just move his retirement date forward a bit. They'd already begun to train his replacement so the department would be fine. But before he did that, he was going to use everything at his disposal to find out what happened to Allison.

Allison wasn't pleased to hear that Nate would be gone for weeks, but knew that he needed to go back to Kentucky and deal with his life back there. Once she heard his plans, she was happy she'd decided to stay at the main house, the idea of staying out there in that old cabin alone frightened her. As much as she tried to move forward with her life, she was still having those haunting flashes of memory and the thought of being alone during one of those episodes was frightening.

At least now, if she had one, there was almost always someone around. The cabin, while perfectly adequate was a little rough as well. She hadn't seen Donovan and Elizabeth's cabin, but if it was anything like the one Nate had moved into, she could understand Elizabeth's wish for a new one.

When Nate left a few days later, she was sad to see him go, but it was something that had to be done. Plus he'd promised to spend some of that time trying to figure out who she was, as much as she'd miss him, she really wanted to solve the mystery. She still felt the fear, was still sure that she was in danger, but she wanted more than anything else to be able to move forward with Nate. That wasn't going to happen as long as she couldn't remember what that threat was, or where it might be coming from.

*****

Matt slammed the barn door open, scaring the horses and the men inside. He stalked down the walkway between the stalls and slammed a stack of papers onto the table. "Do you two want to know what I just found out?" He said, through clenched teeth. It took everything he had not to yell, but the horses didn't like it so he controlled himself.

Curley and Gus came slowly out of the stalls they'd been cleaning, neither of them liked horses so this was a punishment. Matt treated them like kids, dangerous kids, but kids none the less. "It seems that our little mess has just gotten messier. Evidently Allison managed to come back from the dead and board that flight to Las Vegas." He said, letting the words sink in.

"Oh." Curley said, not sure what was coming but knowing it was going to be bad.

"I'd like to beat the shit out of both of you and dump you're bodies out there, but instead you're going to Las Vegas." He said, then seeing the look that came over both their faces added, "Before you even start thinking about the good time you're going to have, let me set you straight. You're going to spend every hour of every day looking for Allison."

"But boss, Vegas is a big place. How are we going to find her? It's impossible." Gus said, then shut his mouth when Curley elbowed him in the side.

"You're going to take her picture and hit the streets, you idiot. Offer a reward, do whatever you have to, but find the bitch. Don't hurt her either, I want her in one piece, unharmed. Once you have her, secure her until I can come deal with her."

Gus opened his mouth to ask another question, but shut it again when Curley elbowed him again. "Yes, sir. When do we leave?" Curley said instead.

"You've got three hours, and if hear that you're doing anything besides looking for Allison, I'll come to Vegas and kill you myself. I'll have eyes on you, you know Vegas is my hometown." Matt said, sneering at them. "Don't cross me or you'll be sorry."

"No sir. We wouldn't dream of it. We'll find her, you'll see." Curley said, practically bowing to Matt.

"Screw this one up and you're done. Understand?" Matt said, then after a nod from both men turned and strode up the walkway again. "Your plane tickets and hotel reservation are on the table, don't miss you're flight."

Back outside, Matt took a deep breath, why he'd ever saddled himself with those two idiots he'd never know. But he was stuck with them now, hopefully they'd surprise him and find that dumb bitch. She'd all but ruined his life, it was beyond him how she'd survived that night, gotten on a plane, then disappeared. But Vegas was a big place and a good place to disappear if you wanted to, but she couldn't hide from him for long.

Vegas was his home, he'd been raised on the streets, knew every scam there was and ran most of them. Those street had been his training for the biggest scam of his life, he'd learned his lesson well, he thought looking at the acres of prime grazing land that now belonged to him. So what if it wasn't legally his, for now he was the owner and only Allison could ruin that for him.

She'd been suspicious of him from the very beginning, but when he'd produced the new will her mother had supposedly written just days before her death from cancer, she'd become even more suspicious. He knew that she'd contacted an attorney to look at the will, but he'd been careful to make the forgery look real, it would take months for them to figure out it wasn't real.

By then he'd planned to be long gone, prize money in his pocket, but then Allison had found him in the barn. In some ways this might actually work in his favor, now he'd be free to stay on at Barrington Fields, the owner of a property that was worth millions. He'd have to do something about all the debt he'd accumulated against the property, but winning the Triple Crown would go a long way towards paying them off.

The more he thought about it, the more he decided that he should have just arranged for Allison to have an accident as soon as her mother was dead. He hadn't been sure that he wanted to add murder to his long list of sins, but found that he'd felt little guilt when he'd thought she was dead. Guess it wasn't that hard to kill after all. Plus now he'd get his hands on her, just thinking about it made his crotch tighten in anticipation.

But while he was waiting, he had to find her car, it couldn't have just disappeared. Unless she'd pushed it into a lake somewhere, it had to be somewhere between here and the airport. He'd start with the airport, which was the most logical place for it to be, then work his way backward. If they found her before he found the car, he'd just make her tell him where it was, then he'd get rid of it for good, along with her.

Just thinking about how much fun it was going to be lightened his mood, once word went out in Vegas that he was looking for her, there was no way she'd escape him. Then he'd fulfill his fantasy, dispose of her body and live in luxury for the rest of his life. He could just see it all now.

*****

Nate had known that it would be hard returning to his parent's house, but hadn't realized just how hard it was going to be. He'd left right after the funeral and walking into the house, a staggering wave of grief hit him. He could still smell his mother's perfume in the air, he took a deep breath then remembered that she was gone. Back in Colorado this had seemed a simple chore, pack up the house then sell it or rent it. But looking around him, he knew that it wouldn't be quite that easy.

His grief still fresh and painful, he decided that the house would have to wait for another day. He'd go home, his own house while full of memories, wouldn't trigger such grief. Tomorrow would be soon enough to make some decisions about what he wanted to do from here. What he really wanted was to get home and call Allison, he'd been gone less that twenty four hours, but he missed her already.

She'd offered to come with him, knowing that he might need some moral support, but he'd refused. "There's no way I'm letting you come with me. Have you forgotten that someone tried to kill you? We have no idea who it was or why, you could be walking into danger. I'm not letting you do that, I'll be fine. We can talk every day."

"I could keep a low profile, wait in the car a lot, whatever it takes."

"No way, I'd love to have you with me, but I'm not putting you in danger."

Now he wished he'd let her come, it would have been nice to curl up in his big bed with her. He'd never shared that bed with a woman, to him bringing a woman into his home and his bed was a big commitment, and there'd been no one in his life that important in a long time. But if Allison had been here, he'd have given her a key.

The next morning he went straight to the police station, avoiding the house completely, knowing that he still wasn't ready to face it yet. He spent the day getting caught up on the cases he'd left behind and arranging for his official retirement. As long as he was home, he'd have to spend some time on the job, but he'd also take some time to work on Allison's case. From Colorado he'd had little hope of conducting any type of investigation, but in person he'd be able to make some progress.

His first stop of the morning was his captain's office, a genial man, who'd risen to the top of the chain through hard work and smarts. Nate wanted to run the details of Allison's case by him. After he'd gotten Nate settled, offering coffee and doughnuts, he looked at Nate appraising his frame of mind.

"How are you handling everything since your mother's passing?" Captain Marlow asked, skipping small talk.

"Well, I thought I was doing okay when I was in Colorado, but coming home had stirred the pain up again. I'm sure it's going to get easier with time."

"So, you like it out there in Colorado? I never did understand what took you all the way out there, and in the middle of winter no less."

"That's a long story and part of the reason I wanted to see you today." Nate said, preparing himself to tell the story start to finish. When he'd finished, Captain Marlow looked at him, then spun in his chair to gaze out the window, a sure sign he was thinking.

"Since there's no missing person's report and you have only her first name, I'd start from the airport where we know she was cognizant enough to board a plane. Have you looked into how she managed to lose all her identification after she boarded the plane?"

"No, I hadn't thought of that. She would've had to have some identification to get on the plane. I wonder how she got to the airport, if she took a taxi there might be a record. If she drove, what happened to her car?" Nate continued to look at the case from all the angles, happy to finally be able to do more than make phone calls from another state.

"Looks like you've got some work to do, you're going to need some help. I can't spare anyone, but I do have a private investigator who could do some of the leg work." Captain Marlow said, handing Nate a business card.

"A private investigator? Have you lost your mind?" Nate said, shocked.

"No, meet this guy. You'll see. He can help, he's good. Sometimes, he can get information that we can't. It can't hurt to give him a call." Captain Marlow said, giving Nate one of those looks that said you better take my advice.

Nate left the meeting with the private investigator feeling positive, Captain Marlow's description of the man had been spot on. He'd asked the right questions and suggested following the same investigative paths Nate had been considering. He'd hired him on the spot, giving a sizable retainer and generous traveling expenses. He'd explore how Allison had gotten to the airport, while Nate would make the rounds of the small police departments around the state to see if anyone had been looking for her but not filed a missing person's report.

His hope was that someone had tried to report Allison missing but was refused, it happen more then he liked to admit. Officers with too much on their plates not taking the time to give these cases the attention they needed. He'd probably been guilty of the same in the past. It took far longer than Nate would have hoped, to get the investigation going properly, after nearly a week in Kentucky, he had very little to show for the time he'd spent away from Allison.

They had been video chatting every night since he'd been gone, but it just wasn't the same as being there with her. Sometimes it was even more difficult to see her and not be able to touch her, but now that the investigation was in full swing, he had time to turn his attention to more personal matters and his parent's house. He'd been packing his own house up over the past week, a chore that wasn't all that difficult, since he had little besides his clothes and some electronics.

His parent's house was a different story, he'd been making short visits over the last week and discovered that not only would he have to deal with all the furniture, but every closet and drawer was full of stuff. In one closet, he'd found an antique vase packed inside stacks and stacks of old newspapers. He'd opened one drawer and found his mother's pearls mixed in with old nails and bolts, clearly this was a job he'd have to do himself.

It was a daunting to have to face all that alone, it would take weeks to sort and pack everything in the house. After a first frustrating day of moving from one task to another, he realized that he had no idea how to even go about the job. He needed an expert, but the last thing he wanted to do was bring in some stranger to help him sort his parent's belongings. Not for the first time, he wished that Allison could have come with him.

That night as soon as his face appeared on the screen, Allison knew that it had been a hard day for Nate. She knew he'd been out to the house to begin packing and sorting. "So, how did it go today?" She asked, wishing she could be there with him.

"Not so great. I don't know where to start. It's such a big job, but I don't exactly want to bring a stranger in. Maybe I should just wait until you can come and help me." Nate said, feeling sorry for himself.

"You know I would be happy to do that, I wish I could be there with you now, but you know I can't and it might be awhile before I'll be able to." Allison said, gently.

"I know I should just get this over with, it's not safe to leave all this stuff just sitting here. It would be easier if I could just pull the valuables out and lock the doors, but everything is everywhere. No, I'll just have to stick it out and get it done." Nate said, feeling better talking to Allison.

No matter how hard the day had been, talking to Allison always made him feel better. If he really got organized it wouldn't be so bad. He'd just keep thinking about Allison. That alone would make the job easier, he'd just have to push though and get it finished. Knowing that when he was finished he could go home to Allison helped too.

As soon as Allison got off the phone with Nate, she went in search of Garrett, it was getting late but she knew he'd still be up. What had been a record winter for snow fall, had turned into one of the wettest springs in recent history. The region had been experiencing a mild drought, but what had at first seemed like a godsend had quickly turned into a serious threat as the snow had continued to fall.

Garrett and the other boys had been worrying about spring runoff for weeks, even though to Allison it looked like the mountain was still frozen solid. But if they were concerned, there was good reason. She found him, as she knew she would, at his big desk in the library, pouring over forest service and topographical maps.

When he saw her and the concerned look on her face, he immediately put aside the maps and gave her his full attention. Over the last few weeks, Allison had finally been able to get past her fear of the Terrell brothers, especially Garrett who appeared gruff on the outside but was as soft as a kitten on the inside. He'd been her rock with Nate gone, helping her make sense of the flashes of memory that still plagued her.

"Allison, what are you still doing up? Is everything okay?" Garrett asked, concern creasing his handsome features.

"No I'm worried about Nate, he's out there in Kentucky all alone, trying to sort through his parent's lives. He needs someone with him. I think I should go, it can't be that much of a risk. We can't just leave him out there alone." She said, close to tears.

Garrett gave her a few seconds to get control of her emotions, "I agree with Nate, it's too dangerous for you to go out there. How about I go instead?" He suggesting, suddenly liking the idea.

"You would do that?" She asked, knowing that he had responsibilities on the ranch and was worried about the flood that everyone feared was a foregone conclusion.

"He's my brother, if he needs help then I'm going to be there for him." Garrett simply said.

"What will Sabrina say?"

"Probably when do we leave?" He said, laughing.

Allison couldn't help herself, she jumped up from where she was sitting, ran around the desk and gave Garrett a big hug. He was shocked at first, but then hugged her back.

Sabrina choose that moment to walk into the room and Allison quickly backed away from Garrett. Instead of being mad at what she'd seen, she simply smiled and asked, "What are we celebrating?"

"Nate's having a hard time out in Kentucky sorting his parent's things, I've just offered our services since Allison can't go." Garrett said, flashing Sabrina one of those smiles he knew she couldn't resist.

"And were you going to ask me about this at some point?" she asked, hands on her hips.

"Well, honestly I only offered my services, but somehow I can't imagine you're going to let me out of your sight for any length of time, so..."

"Darn right. When do we leave?"

Garrett and Allison burst into laughter. "Told you." He said.

Garrett decided this was one of those times that using their private jet was called for, so by the next night when Allison saw Nate's face on her computer screen, Garrett and

Sabrina were in the background. Sabrina had taken over and they'd already come up with a plan to clean out the house and get Nate back to Colorado.

"I can't believe you sent them out here." Nate said, tears in his eyes.

"Well, they're your family. I couldn't be there so I sent the next best thing."

## Chapter 9

Garrett and Sabrina stayed with Nate for two weeks, helping him with the monumental task. Garrett had taken one look at the antiques and made a phone call to Donovan and by the next morning they had an expert on hand to deal with the furniture and art, some of which was extremely old and valuable. It was clear to Nate that for now he'd have to store the contents of the house in a secure facility until he decided what to do with it all.

Nate hesitated with getting rid of anything, so many of the pieces came with stories about how they'd become part of his family's history, some dating back to before the Civil War. In the end, he decided to keep everything, there was just too much history to turn his back on.

When he talked to Allison about it, she agreed with his decision. "That's still your history, whether it's from you father's side of the family or your mother's, those are the people that made you the man you are today. Just because the man who you thought of as your father wasn't biologically your father, doesn't mean that a piece of him doesn't exist in you."

"Perfectly said, as always, my love." He said, thanking fate again for sending him Allison.

Allison's heart skipped a beat when she heard him call her his love, but she knew that it was only a figure of speech. They hadn't talked about love and for many reasons she was happy about that. No matter how much she wanted to pretend otherwise, she had another life out there somewhere just waiting to possibly destroy the one she was working to build now.

By the time Garrett and Sabrina left, taking his mother's jewelry and some of the more precious art work with them, both houses were empty and closed up. Nate didn't know how long they'd remain that way, but he couldn't bear to part with either property, both had been in the family for generations. Over the course of his lifetime, he'd put plenty of blood, sweat, and tears into keeping them in the best shape he could.

His efforts had been worth it, both properties were very valuable, but apparently he didn't need the money as Garrett had pointed out when they'd discussed the possibility of him selling. His words had echoed Allison's with the added information about what his disbursement from the trust would be.

"I'm sorry. How much?" He'd been shocked when Garrett had mentioned a number.

"You heard me. Four times a year you get a check." Garrett had laughed, "guess that's even more proof that you're not out for the money."

"Well, then I'm keeping the Kentucky properties, it makes no sense to sell them. Who knows, I might want to come back here someday. Maybe I'll spend my winters here where its warm." He laughed, feeling relieved to have finally made a decision that included keeping his family home.

Nate desperately wanted to go home with them, but he felt he'd be able to investigate better in person, so he turned his attention back to Allison. The private detective had followed a few leads, but it was really a matter of canvasing the airport, talking to bus drives, taxi drivers, and tow truck drivers. The airport didn't keep records of cars that had been towed, considering them the possession of the impound lot once they'd been hooked up.

None of the police departments he'd talked to had been of any help, but he thought he might branch out further, Kentucky wasn't a big state. Allison could have come from any of the surrounding states, although considering her injuries, he felt sure she hadn't driven very far. Still a few more weeks pursuing leads might put something in motion, he'd long ago learned that stirring things up was often the only way to solve an old crime.

Allison's attack was soon becoming an old crime and they were always harder to solve, he owed it to both of them to hang out for a few more weeks and see if he could come up with anything new. He packed what belongings he had left in a rented car and headed out, making a wide sweep in a circle around the airport.

He stopped at police stations, bus stations, and gas stations showing Allison's picture to anyone who would look. After two weeks, he arrived back where he'd started and decided it was time to go back to Colorado. Spring was just beginning to arrive and he didn't want to miss the mountains coming to life. Besides that, he missed Allison with what was becoming an almost painful longing, they'd been apart for almost six weeks and he missed her more every day.

As Nate was boarding a plane, thinking about Allison, Matt was in the parking lot of the airport thinking about her as well. However, his thoughts were not as pleasant as Nate's. With every other breath he was cursing her, wishing he'd taken care of her much sooner. It gave him some comfort to imagine what he'd do to her when he found her, with each passing day it became more of an obsession.

But she deserved everything he was going to do to her when he caught up with her. For three solid weeks he'd been searching parking lots and impound lots for her silver car. How an entire car could disappear, he had no idea, but eventually he'd find it and her. Besides cussing Allison and imagining her demise, he had some vivid fantasies of what he was going to do to Curley and Gus once they found Allison.

Sometimes he was so frustrated he just wanted to have them eliminated, but then he'd have to bring in someone new and he just didn't want the hassle. Of course he did have to admit that they'd been doing the job he sent them to do. His contacts had reported seeing them all over town showing the bitch's picture and offering a reward for any information about her.

But, all those efforts as well as those of his contacts had turned up nothing. He'd even hired a guy to try and trace her electronically but nothing had popped up. Now he was beginning to become desperate. He couldn't figure out how she'd been able to disappear so completely, she couldn't have changed her appearance that much, not without surgery. He knew that was out of the question because he made sure she had as little money as possible.

It had been one of the ways he kept her under his thumb, he'd promised to pay her a wage for working on the farm, but only paid her when she threw a fit. How she'd managed to pay for her plane ticket he had no idea, but at the time, he'd just been happy that she was leaving for a few days. Now he was questioning how she'd managed it, then it occurred to him that she might have had some help.

Finally giving up for the day, he shoved the papers that had been on the seat next to him onto the floor in frustration, it was exhausting spending everyday trolling parking lots, sometimes avoiding security guards who became suspicious. The papers had landed on the floor with the fax about Allison's flight on top, it was then that he noticed that the flight had stopped in Denver.

Suddenly, he knew what she'd done. She'd gotten off that plane in Denver, never even made it to Las Vegas, he'd been searching for her in the wrong place. Feeling stupid for not seeing it before now, he cursed some more, adding another punishment to the long list he had planned for Allison. It was exactly what he would have done, had in fact done in the past.

Driving back to the cheap motel he'd rented close to the airport, he called Curley and Gus and told them to come home. All the time they'd spent in Las Vegas had been worthless, what was worse he'd been away from the horses much too long. If they didn't get another injection in the next few days, all his hopes for that Triple Crown win would go up in smoke, the race was a little over a month away and he needed that money.

It was time to come up with a new plan to find Allison, but more importantly he needed to win those races to save the farm. Allison or no Allison it was his for now and he had every intention of holding on to it.

*****

Nate's flight landed on time and he was on the road within an hour, Allison had wanted to come get him but he'd refused, remembering the last time she'd gotten into a car. They'd decided to run into town for some groceries, the roads had been clear so Allison had talked him into letting her drive. She was sure that she remembered how and wanted to test her theory.

She did fine for the first few minutes, but then she'd begun to get a head ache, followed by vivid images of her driving a car and wiping blood off her head with a towel. She'd slammed on the brakes, the memory of digging through a suitcase for something to wipe the blood off her face as she drove playing clearly in her mind.

Nate had wrapped his arms around her as she sat, head in hands watching the scene unfold in her mind. Instead of the usual flashes, this was a complete picture, a complete memory. It had scared her so bad, they'd sat in the car for almost an hour before she could even move from her seat. Nate had held her the entire time, rocking her until she stopped shaking.

Looking back at it later, they had both agreed that it was a positive thing that she'd had a complete memory, but also that she shouldn't try to drive again. He didn't completely trust her not to get in the car anyway, so he'd booked an earlier flight and would surprise her by getting there early.

It was mid-afternoon when he finally pulled into the ranch, it looked nothing like the last time he was here. The snow drifts were six feet high in places, but showed signs of melting, rivers of water running down the side of the road evidence of warmer weather. He was surprised how warm it was when he stepped out of the car, it'd been warm in Denver, but he'd expected it to be cold this high in the mountains.

Stretching, he looked around, feeling happy to be back at the ranch. A lot had happened since he left, but it felt good to be back. This time driving up the road, he'd realized he felt like he was coming home, a nice feeling for someone who had been alone only a few months ago. When his eyes finally swiveled to the house he saw Allison in the kitchen window.

Just the sight of her standing there was enough to make his heart beat a little faster. Suddenly, it felt like he couldn't get to her fast enough. He came stomping through the house, past the living room, through the dining room and into the kitchen, swept Allison up in his arms and kissed her.

She was so shocked to find herself in his arms being kissed she almost hit him in the head with the rolling pin she'd been holding. But within seconds, she realized who was holding her and dropped the rolling pin and threw her flour covered arms around him. After he'd kissed her breathless, she looked at him, smiling.

"Where did you come from?" She asked, slapping him on the arm.

"I wanted to surprise you." He said, hardly able to control his urge to grab her up and kiss her again.

"Well, you succeeded. I should be mad at you, but I'm too happy to see you to be mad right now." She said, kissing him.

By then all the family had found their way into the kitchen, his brothers were making catcalls while the women were wiping away tears. "Very romantic, Nate." Donovan said, coming over to slap him on the back.

"Good to see you home." Sebastian said, following suit.

"Any news?" Garrett said, always the practical one.

After they'd all greeted him, Sabrina ushered everyone out of the room. Nate looked around the kitchen which was covered in cookies, cakes, and other pastries. Then he looked at Allison who although wearing an apron was covered in flour, it was in her hair, on her face, and there was even a hand print on her butt were she'd wiped her hands.

"What have you been doing?" He asked, wondering what he'd missed.

"Well, we've been cooped up inside for weeks. I needed something to keep me busy, and I've always wanted to learn to bake. I started binge watching baking shows when you were gone, and one night I just came down here and started baking."

"I didn't know you liked to bake." He said, amazed at the array of baked goods she'd assembled.

"Honestly, I didn't know either. But something about it just feels right." Allison said, rushing to take a batch of cookies out of the oven before they burned.

"Does it feel like something you used to do?" He asked, taking a warm cookie when she offered it.

"No, it feels like something new. This all looks good, but you should have seen some of my first attempts. Baking at high altitude takes some finesses, but I've got it now. I'm actually making money on all this." She said proudly.

"Wow, that's great." Nate said, a little hurt that she hadn't told him about all this.

"I'm sorry I didn't tell you, but it all happened so fast, what was a hobby has suddenly turned into something I can do to support myself. It's a little scary." She said, wishing Nate would say something supportive.

Nate realized he was being ridiculous, it's not like he'd expected her to sit around doing nothing while he was in Kentucky, but this was a whole new side of Allison he hadn't seen before. "Well, I guess I better see what all the fuss is about." He said, taking a big bite of the cookie.

To say that it was the best cookie he'd ever eaten would have been an understatement, it was crisp on the outside but chewy in the center, and melted in his mouth as he chewed. There was a burst of flavor in every bite, leaving him wanting more. He took another bite and said with his mouth full, "Oh my God, this is the best thing I've ever eaten."

Allison just smiled and handed him a cream puff covered in caramel, which he stuffed in his mouth in one bite. When he'd chewed and swallowed, he looked around the room appreciating all that she'd accomplished while he'd been gone.

"You taught yourself to make all this?" He asked, taking another cookie off the tray.

"I had some help from Cinthia and Daphne, but basically yes."

His mind had immediately gone to that empty store front in town, visions of a coffee bar serving Allison's baked goods. It would make money hand over fist in a tourist town like Pleasant Valley. But before he could voice his plans to Allison, she took off her apron and grabbed his hand.

"I've also been working on a little project in your cabin. I hope you like it." She said, handing him his jacket and stepping into a pair of rubber boots. "You'll want to put on a pair of those, it's a mess out there." She added pointing to a row of identical boots.

They sloshed though the mud to Nate's cabin, although he hadn't really begun to think of it that way. He'd only stayed in it for a few nights before he'd gone to Kentucky. When he'd been thinking about home, he'd been thinking about Allison's bed, but he'd have to get used to this being home from now on. When they got to the cabin, Allison opened the door with a flourish and pushed Nate thought.

What he saw amazed him, the cabin had been completely refurnished, using his favorite pieces from both his house and his parents. Somehow Allison had managed to pick the exact pieces he would have picked for himself, including his desk and the leather couch that was his favorite. He'd imagined making love to Allison on that couch plenty of times when he'd been away, falling asleep thinking of her luscious curves.

Now it was in his living room, just waiting for that fantasy to become a reality. But before he could grab her and drag her down onto the couch, she said, "Well, what do you think?" Then seeing the look in his eyes, she sucked in a breath, her stomach tightening with desire.

"It's wonderful, exactly the way I would have done it. But why did you do it?"

"I know you decided to leave all your furniture back in Kentucky, but the more I thought about it the more I realized that some of it should be here. Sabrina helped me pull it off." She said, happy to see that he liked it.

"Naturally Sabrina would have been involved." He said, smiling. "Now, I've been having some especially interesting thoughts about you and that couch."

Nate pulled her over to the couch and down onto his lap, his mouth finding hers in a possessive kiss, that had her head spinning. They'd been apart for a long time, but the minute his mouth captured hers, she felt like nothing had separated them. Her body responded to his, as his mouth ravaged hers, like he was trying to make up for lost time.

He pulled her shirt over her head and threw it across the room, then removed his. She pressed her breasts against his hard chest, thrilled to feel his heart beating as rapidly as hers. But before things could go farther, she had one more surprise for Nate.

"Hold on, I still have one more thing to show you." She said, pulling him up from the couch. "I'm a little nervous about this one."

He followed her into the bedroom, where he found his bed. It filled almost the entire room, but Allison had covered it with a blue silk bedspread and lots of big fat pillows. It looked exactly like he'd always imagined it should look. He stopped right inside the doorway, a little sound of surprise escaping his lips.

"You brought my bed out here." He said, shocked at how good it looked in the little room.

"It's such a wonderful bed, obviously very old. I couldn't resist when I saw it in the pictures." She said, hoping that he was happy, but unable to read the look on his face.

Nate couldn't have been more pleased. Taking her by the hand, he led her over to the bed and sat her down on the edge. There was no way she could know what this bed meant to him, but he was going to explain to her why she'd done exactly the right thing.

"This bed has been in my family for generations on my father's side. When he died my mother insisted I take it. I bought a new mattress and set it up in my house thinking that someday I'd bring the woman I love home to it. But it never happened, no matter how much I liked a woman, I couldn't imagine making love to her in this bed. When I walked into my room and saw the bed I knew that you were the woman I was supposed to share it with. It was like my father was giving us his blessing."

"Nate, I had no idea. I just loved the bed and wanted you to have it here." She said, looking into his blue eyes, thinking how lucky she was to have such a sensitive man.

"I think now we should make this our bed." He said, pulling her to him and down on the bed.

## Chapter 10

Allison jumped up, "Nate I'm covered with flour and who knows what else, I have to take a shower." She said, stripping off the rest of her clothes. "Wait right here, I'll be right back."

"I'm right behind you, I've been traveling all day, besides do you really think I'm going to let you take a shower alone. I'm not letting you out of my sight for at least the next forty eight hours, so you'd better get used to the sight of me.

Nate actually beat Allison into the shower and was already washing his hair when she got in. This wasn't the first time they'd taken a shower together, but the sexual tension between them could be felt in the air, this would not be a normal shower. When Allison stepped into the shower, Nate had his eyes closed, head back, rinsing his hair. She placed her hands on his hard chest, then lowered them to take his erection in her hands, making him gasp with pleasure.

Nate finished rinsing his hair, then swung Allison into the steaming water. She bent her head back, letting the water wash over her long hair, enjoying the heat soaking into her tired muscles. Stepping forward she opened her eyes to see

Nate staring at her, his eyes that shade of blue that she loved so much.

He turned her around, the water rushing across her breasts and down her legs, grabbed the shampoo and washed her hair. He'd never done that before and she found it more sensual than she would have ever imagined. When he turned her to rinse her hair, she let the water wash over her, desire beginning to coil deep inside her.

Nate took the soap in his hands and began to rub it over her body starting at her feet and working his way up. When he came to the juncture of her thighs, he slid over the area, making Allison whimper. But soon his hands were on her swollen breasts, slick with soap. He rubbed her until she was moaning with pleasure, her legs barely able to support her.

He turned her in the shower again, letting the water cascade across her breasts, the soap bubbles disappearing down the drain. He soaped her back, then let his hands drift lower, until he had each of her full cheeks in his hands. Allison could hardly breathe, her legs shaking with anticipation when he finally ran his slick soapy hand between her legs.

Allison cried out with the pleasure of finally feeling his hands on her moist flesh. Knowing that if she didn't hang on, she'd sink to her knees in the tub, she bent forward and braced her hands against the wall, spreading her legs as she did. Nate growling with the pleasure of feeling her hot and wet for him, rubbed her clit, positioning her in the shower so the hot water washed over her tender nib.

Her body driving her need, she spread her legs farther as the coil of pleasure became more intense. Nate continued to rub her in gentle circles, spreading heat through her body. She came crying out his name, the spasms rocking her body with their intensity. Before she could even catch her breath, Nate slid his finger deep inside her, stroking her until the pleasure began to coil again.

When her orgasm rushed through her this time, she was sure she couldn't handle any more, but then Nate grabbed her hips and drove himself into her still trembling body. He was impatient, wanting to feel himself deep inside her, he drove himself into her over and over again.

Feeling his own release coming, he pulled out of her and spun her around in the shower, His mouth descended on hers, searing her with another blast of desire. She'd thought she was spent, but feeling the raw desire in Nate's kiss, only increased her need for him, to touch him, taste him, to possess him.

Sinking to her knees she took him in her mouth and massaged him with her tongue, loving the way he grabbed fistfuls of her hair. She could feel his penis getting harder as she licked and teased him, finally taking all of him into her mouth again. Nate began rocking his hips, driving himself into her mouth, deeper each time.

Finally, with a strangled cry, he pulled her to her feet and then picked her up. She wrapped her legs around his hips as he drove himself into her, backing her up against the wall, as he buried himself inside her over and over again. Allison was no longer aware of anything besides Nate and the wonderful things he was doing to her body.

She clung to him, her head thrown back as Nate possessed her as completely as any man ever could. Nate's legs began to shake as his climax came closer, but he still wasn't ready to let go. Setting Allison back on her feet, he knelt down in front of her and spread her legs. With his fingers he spread her folds and bent forward, his tongue finding her clit. Sliding his tongue over the swollen bud, he grabbed her nipples between his finger and thumb and squeezed them, sending her spiraling into a fury of sensation only Nate could create.

Just as she was about to crest on a wave of pleasure, he got to his feet, spun her around, spread her legs and thrust himself into her again. This time, she came with a force that made the world go black for long minutes as she rode the pleasure of his hard cock buried deep inside her, throbbing as he spilled himself inside her, crying her name as he did.

By the time they managed to climb out of the shower, the water had grown cold and they shivered as they jumped into the big bed. Nate dried Allison's hair, then brushed the tangles out, loving the feel of the long silky strands as it slid thought his fingers. When he was finished with her hair, they cuddled up, Allison shocking Nate by putting her cold feet on his legs.

They spoke little, the experience they'd just shared saying everything they needed to say to each other. Finally

Nate broke the silence, "We still haven't made this our bed you know."

"I guess not, but the shower is definitely ours." She said, laughing.

"Well, it just doesn't seem fair that you brought it all the way here and we're just lying here doing nothing." Nate said, sliding his hand between her legs.

"I suppose you're right. What did you have in mind?" She asked, trying to look innocent.

Nate sat up a little, grabbed her by the hips and pulled her on top of him. His erection was pressing suggestively against her opening, begging to be let in. She reached between them, grabbed him and slid him inside her.

"That's exactly what I had in mind." He said, reaching for her.

Late that night, they snuck back over to the main house to clean up the mess Allison had left that afternoon, but when they walked in the door the mess was gone. There was a note on the counter from Sabrina.

*Welcome home Nate, there's dinner in the oven for you guys. Sleep late in the morning if you want.*

They found two huge plates of food in the oven, which they devoured. On the way back to the cabin, Allison grabbed a blueberry pie and two forks, which they ate in bed, then fell asleep in each other's arms. They slept soundly that night both happy to be with the one they loved.

The next morning, they didn't get up to the main house until mid-morning, long after breakfast was over, but everyone was still in the kitchen. When they walked in the door, Donovan and Elizabeth were sitting at the kitchen table, several sets of roughly drawn sketches of their cabin in front of them. It was clear from their body language they were having another discussion about their cabin.

Donovan was the first to spot them, happy for anything that might distract Elizabeth, he said, "Well it's about time you two decided to show up." Then tried to get up from the table.

But Elizabeth was wise to his avoidance tactics, "No way. Sit back down here." She said, then put another sketch in front of him. "I like this one, it would blend in just fine with the others, but would also offer modern conveniences like a bath tub."

"But would also cost a small fortune." He said, pushing it away. "What's wrong with just adding onto the cabin? We could add another room. Make the kitchen bigger. See look at this."

"Nope, it looks like you put two completely different houses together." Elizabeth said, pushing it away.

Nate and Allison had quietly been pouring themselves a cup of coffee, trying not to listen to what was quickly turning into a fight. They looked at each other then turned to look at the couple to find that they were looking at Nate. With a sinking feeling Nate knew he was going to be a part of this discussion whether he liked it or not.

"Want me to take a look. I'm new at this but...."

"Yes, that's exactly what we need, an independent opinion. And let me remind you money is not an issue, no matter what Donovan says." Elizabeth said.

"But it also makes no sense to replace a perfectly good building with a new one." Donovan said, making sure his side was known.

"I think I understand what you both want. Elizabeth wants modern conveniences, the features of a smart house, and added eco friendly features like solar power. Donovan, you want to conserve what is essentially a historic building on the ranch, while keeping costs as low as possible." Nate said, looking from one to the other.

"Exactly." They said in unison, then laughed breaking the tension in the room.

"I'll need a little time to come up with some designs, but I've already been looking at my cabin, wondering how I would, um, redo it for a family." Nate said, looking at Allison, they'd never talked about kids, he'd assumed she'd want some, but you never knew.

Allison blushed, then said, "If your cabin is like Nate's it would be hard to raise a family there, even if you added extra rooms the kitchen is much too small."

"See." Elizabeth said, happy to have another woman's opinion.

"Okay, don't start fighting again. I'll put something together and get back to you right away." Nate said, scooping up all the sketches on the table.

"That wasn't fighting." Sebastian said, from across the room, "you'll know when they're fighting. Hey, Nate as long as you're working up something for them, how about doing our cabin as well. It's just a matter of time before Leslie starts hollering for the same thing." He said, softening his words by pulling her onto his lap as she tried to walk past him to the sink.

"Good save." She said, kissing him.

"Elizabeth, where's the baby?" Allison asked, looking around the room. She'd grown fond of Rebecca over the last few weeks, she was a happy baby which made it easy to love her.

"She's upstairs asleep, she's been running a little fever. I think she might be teething." Elizabeth said, with a frown.

"I thought so too." Cinthia said, walking into the room with Jonathan right behind her. "She was chewing on anything she could get her hands on yesterday."

"I don't know if I'm ready for this, so much for my sweet angel." Elizabeth said, with a groan.

Cinthia patted Elizabeth on the back and crossed the room and to Nate's utter surprise, gave him a hug. "Glad to see you made it home okay. I'm sorry you had to go through that. It must have been difficult." She said, looking up at him.

"Thank you, it certainly helped having Garrett and Sabrina with me, but I am glad to be home." Nate managed to say through his shock.

He looked to Allison, who only smiled, and then to Jonathan who nodded his head in encouragement. Nate was overwhelmed with emotion, suddenly right that second he felt like he was a part of this family. That he had a place here, belonged right here with these people. He still missed his parents, but the world no longer looked like the bleak place it had only months ago.

He sat down at the table, hoping that no one could see his emotion, but naturally Allison was quite aware of what he was feeling. She sat down next to him and took his hand, giving it a squeeze of encouragement. Then sat silently next to him, letting the conversation flow around her.

Garrett and Sabrina had been huddled in the back corner of the room where Sabrina had put her desk. Since the kitchen seemed to be the place that everyone passed through at least once a day she felt that it gave her a better idea of what was happening in the house. Sabrina, besides helping Daphne home-school the kids and running the therapy program, was in charge of the main house.

Although they rarely had house guests, there was a constant stream of people through the house, most of whom ate at least one meal a day there. Lately, the task had become more than she could handle on her own and Allison had been taking on some of those responsibilities as well. They made a good team, and Sabrina had been partially responsible for Allison's interest in baking, encouraging her to try new things.

Garrett walked over to the coffee pot and refilled his cup, then cleared his throat and said, "Since we're all here, I think this might be a good time for a family meeting."

There were groans, but Garrett ignored them. "First, I want to welcome Nate to the family. It was a bit of a shock at first, but now that we've gotten to know you I can see you're a Terrell through and through." He said, then added, "I think it's time you took that ring off the chain and put it on your finger."

Nate had almost forgotten he'd been wearing the ring around his neck, it had become such a part of him. Pulling the chain over his head, he removed the ring and slid it onto his finger. Everyone cheered, then got quiet. "The legal department had taken care of all the paperwork, you are now a full voting member of the board of directors for Terrell Industries."

"What? I didn't know I'd have to do that. I don't know anything about business." Nate stammered.

"Don't worry." Leslie said, "I didn't either. You'll be fine. Everyone on the board is sitting in the room right now."

www.AfroRomanceBooks.com/RomanceBooks

"Oh, okay. I guess." Nate was nearly speechless with shock.

Garrett nodded his head at Donovan giving him the floor. "I don't have much except it looks like Nate's going to be adding a new branch to the business. We're going to have to look into forming our own construction company. If we're going to be renovating cabins, stores, and whatever else Nate has in mind, it may be more financially sound to have our own equipment and employees. Nate you and I can discuss the possibilities later, I'd like your input."

"Sure, just let me know when. I've got free time." Nate said, taking a deep breath, everything was happening really fast, first he was renovating cabins now all of the sudden he was heading up a construction company.

Sebastian was clearly next, "I've heard back from the civil engineer about the lower pasture dam, he seems to think that it's a total loss. That the only way to go is to build an entirely new one."

"But that's not what the engineer last summer told us." Garrett said, gritting his teeth. "We've got to do something and fast. As it is, I'm not sure it's going to hold for spring runoff. Did he have any suggestions for temporarily shoring it up?"

"He seemed unwilling to even consider the possibility, said it would be a total waste of his time. The guy was a total jerk." Sebastian said. Then looked at Nate, "I don't suppose you know anything about building a dam?"

"No, not really." Nate said, "What's the problem?"

"Let me show you." Garrett said, spreading out his maps on the table.

Nate was happy to be distracted by Garrett's maps, his head was spinning with everything he'd just been given. But as he listened, he realized that if the dam at the bottom of the upper pasture was to give, the entire ranch would be under water within minutes. "Explain that all to me again."

By the end of the morning, Nate had suddenly accumulated a long list of things he needed to do. But, all those thing were going to wait for a few days until he'd satisfied his need to be close to Allison. He hadn't been kidding when he said, he wasn't going to let her out of his sight for forty eight hours.

As everyone scattered to their respective responsibilities, Allison looked at Nate, clearly wondering what they were going to do. "Feel like taking a trip to town. I think we need some supplies for the cabin, some food, dishes, pots and pans."

"Okay, that sounds like fun. A shopping spree." Allison said, laughing.

"I guess so." He said, taking her hand.

Several hours later, they arrived home with a car full of supplies and a few treats including a new flat screen television for the bedroom. They had to carry it all the way out to the cabin from the parking lot by the main house and Nate promised himself that the first thing he was going to build was a driveway to the cabin. Maybe a garage that looked like a barn, his mind began to wander with all the possibilities.

While Nate hung the new television in the bedroom, Allison put away the new dishes they'd picked out in town. She had to hand wash them all since the cabin didn't have a dishwasher, making her more on Elizabeth's side than ever. It also occurred to her that there wasn't a washer and dryer either, that meant taking the laundry to the main house or the laundry mat, another point on Elizabeth's side.

Allison was so lost in her thoughts about the Terrell's and their lives, that at first, she didn't notice how quiet it had gotten in the bed room. She was sure that she'd find Nate asleep on the bed or watching some sports program, but instead she found him sketch book in hand leaning against the headboard of the bed.

He was so absorbed in what he was doing, she had time to just study him. His face was relaxed, all trace of the pressures of life gone, the little lines beside his eyes and mouth making him even more handsome. His blonde hair was ruffled and Allison could see a few silvery strands at his temples. Her heart nearly skipped a beat when she realized just how much she loved him.

She hadn't wanted him to leave, but it had actually been a good thing for them. It had slowed things down and allowed them to connect on a deeper level. Sex with Nate was beyond anything she could have imagined, but she also craved the emotional connection that their separation had facilitated. Now that he was back, their desire for one another had reached a more normal level, a level that would allow them to build something more.

She walked further into the room, amused that Nate was so completely absorbed in what he was doing. She laid down on the bed next to him, and threw her leg over his, watching as he sketched. Slowly, he became aware of her, but didn't stop what he was doing. Instead, he began to sketch over the original building, creating a new design that not only kept the integrity of the old, but allowed for the new, pointing out the changes he was making, he walked her though the new design.

Allison listen and watched as Nate turned the little cabin into a proper home, including a small barn for a couple of horses. "That's amazing. It's perfect." She said, impressed.

"Well, it still needs some work. That's just a rough sketch, I'll have to use my computer to create real designs, but you can see how it would look." Nate said, setting the sketch book aside, suddenly a little embarrassed by her praise.

"It looked good to me." She said, sitting up to give him a kiss, knowing when to leave something alone. He'd come to see how talented he was soon enough. She'd seen some of his designs when she'd moved his stuff from the main house and he was very talented.

She started to pull away, but he grabbed her and rolled her onto her back, "I was going to ask what was for dinner, but I think I might want my desert first." The look of love in her eyes minutes ago had awakened his passion, he needed her now, needed to feel the love radiating between them.

So much had happened today that he needed to feel connected to her in the most primal way. When their bodies were joined, the rest of the world and its problems faded into the background. For those few precious stolen moments all he had to think about was Allison and the passion she'd brought to his life, a passion he'd thought he'd never find.

# Chapter 11

Later that night after they'd made frozen pizza for dinner, one of the treats they'd brought home with them. Allison was curled up in Nate's arms in the big bed, while they watched an old black and white movie on television. They'd discovered they both liked old movies, the sappier the better. One of Allison's favorites was just finishing, as always the tears were streaming down her cheeks.

Laughing she sat up, wiping the tears away with the heel of her hands. Nate reached over and handed her a tissue, which she used to mop up the rest of the tears. Suddenly Allison realized that not only had she remembered the movie, but she remembered watching it with her mother when she was a little girl.

Nate, seeing the strange look cross her face, was suddenly concerned. He knew that look, it meant that she was remembering something. "What's wrong?" He asked, sitting up and pulling her into his arms.

"I remember that movie." She said, pointing to the T.V. "And I remember watching it with my mother when I was a little girl. My mother loved old movies, that's why I do." She said, starting to hyperventilate.

"Okay, take a deep breath. This is good." He said, rubbing her back.

"I'm scared." She said, burying her face in his shirt. "Those other memories are there, just waiting to come out. What's going to happen when they do?"

"Hey." He said, raising her chin so he could look into her eyes. "I'm going to be right here with you when they do. Nothing you remember can hurt you and if you remember who did this to you, I can guarantee you he's going to be sorry."

Allison had been avoiding thinking about what else she'd remember, like a husband somewhere or even some kids. "Nate, have you ever been married. We've never talked about your past." She said, deciding that now was the time to have this discussion.

"I was, but it was a long time ago. It didn't work out, she thought I was her ticket out of the small town we lived in. I had planned to stay, help take care of my parents, settle down there and have kids of my own. We parted ways after only six months. Last I heard, she was in the city still single and happy." He said, shrugging his shoulders.

Allison was silent for a long time, happy that there wasn't some other woman out there with designs on Nate. "What are we going to do if I have someone out there?" She whispered, hating to say the words, but relieved she finally had.

"Well, the way I see it, if there's someone out there that you're supposed to belong to, they haven't done a very good job of taking care of you and they don't deserve to have you." He said, then added, "But if there is, I'm going to fight for you. What we have is special, don't tell me you don't see that. Maybe this was fates only way of bringing us together." He said, a pleading look in his eyes.

"I don't think there's anyone out there looking for me and that makes me sad." She said, looking down, embarrassed.

Nate kissed her on the temple, "Well, if you disappear tomorrow I can think of a lot of people who will be out looking for you. You're not alone, you have me and the Terrell's, who already consider you family. So no matter what happens, you know you have people who love you and will protect you." Nate said, his words soothing Allison's fears.

They sat in silence for a long time, his arms wrapped around her trembling body. Nate broke the silence, "Jonathan said the Terrell men are especially protective of the women they love. I wasn't sure what he mean until now."

Allison heard his words but wasn't sure that he knew what he'd just said. "What did you say?" She asked, looking up into his impossibly blue eyes.

"You mean the part about loving you. I thought that was obvious, but I thought I'd say it out loud just in case you didn't know for sure. Allison, I love you and always will. I want you here with me, sharing that cabin I've been designing. We'll get through this, one step at a time. Any man out there who thinks he's going to take you away from me is going to have a fight on his hands." His said, his mouth coming down on hers in a kiss so possessive Allison felt it in her soul.

This must be what it feels like to belong to someone she thought as Nate slowly undressed her, murmuring words of love into her ear as he made love to her more gently than he ever had before. When he entered her, she felt complete, whole for the first time in months. Secure in the knowledge that Nate's heart belonged to her and only her.

"I love you too Nate." She said over and over again, clinging to him as the tears ran down her cheeks.

They couldn't have known that right then, the man who would try to take Allison from him was planning his move in his quest to punish her. Matt had been forced to attend to business at the farm, with race day fast approaching he had to make sure his investment was going to pay off. He pushed the Allison problem to the back of his mind. She was clearly hiding from him and posed no immediate threat.

That didn't stop him from nursing his fantasies of what he would do to her when he finally got his hands on her, which he was sure would happen eventually. Once he'd secured his horse's spot in the Kentucky Derby which was still weeks away, he began calling what contacts he had in Denver. Now that he knew she was there for sure, he'd send Curley and Gus out there to search for her.

It wouldn't be as easy as Vegas, but with some luck, they'd track her down. He'd given up looking for her car, if it hadn't been found by now, it wasn't going to be found. Waiting was never his strong suit, but at least he'd be waiting in the luxury of the plantation house on the property. Eventually, Allison would be found and he could close this chapter once and for all, and have a little fun in the process.

*****

As spring came to the Rockies, the snow turned to rain and the mountains began to thaw, only the highest peaks seemed unaffected by the warmer weather. Nate had so much on his plate that he hardly noticed what was happening around him. Weeks passed, his designs for the cabins were almost finished, but he was nervous to show them to the family.

He'd also been working on the problems with the dam, although it wasn't something he'd studied, he had some friends at the university who were working on the problem for them, not only designing a new structure, but emergency plans to fix the current one before the worst of the flooding started. Time was running out, so he'd been learning as much as he could about dams.

Thanks to Elizabeth, who'd served Allison's pastries at a town council meeting, what had once been something to keep her occupied, had suddenly turned into a business, the demand for her pastries and cookies had become overwhelming. She suddenly found herself with more orders than she could fill. The kitchen looked like a bomb had hit, every counter covered with dirty dishes, flour and powdered sugar. The dining room table was covered with sweet sugary confections waiting to be delivered by the kid she'd been forced to hire a week ago.

Allison stood surveying the mess in the kitchen when Sabrina came into the room, unable to hide the gasp of horror at the mess. "I know, I think I've outgrown the kitchen." Allison said, "I've started something that's gotten out of control."

"I hate to say this right now, but Allison you have to get out of my kitchen." Sabrina said, pointing to the door.

Allison laughed, "Would you like me to clean up the mess first?"

"That might be nice. But seriously, I want you to go into town tomorrow and find yourself some retail space. There's bound to be something that will work, we'll get you whatever you need to get things going."

"But..." Allison stammered.

"It's a wise business investment Allison. We'll figure out the money side of it later, now clean this up and stay out." Sabrina said, hugging Allison on the way out the door.

She cleaned the kitchen up in record time, thinking that there was still time that afternoon to get into town and see what she could find. Questioning Sabrina's decision was a waste of time, she knew all too well how difficult it was to change Sabrina's mind once she'd made it up. Instead, she was going to take the offer and open a pastry shop.

Not even thinking about what she was doing, she ran back to Nate's cabin where most of her clothes were, quickly changed her flour covered clothes, grabbed his keys and was out the door. Before she knew it, she was pulling into Pleasant Valley wondering why the town looked different to her. She'd been here just the day before, nothing could have changed since then.

Pulling into the parking lot at the park, she looked down Main Street trying to figure out what was different. Then it hit her, she'd driven into town without even thinking about it, she'd jumped in the car and took off. She hadn't even said goodbye to Nate, who was as usual working in the library with Garrett. Feeling ridiculous, she dug her phone out of the pocket of her jeans and called Nate.

"Hi, um...." She wasn't sure what to say.

"What's wrong? Where are you? I've been frantic, I went looking for you and couldn't find you. Sabrina said you jumped in the car and took off." Nate said, clearly past the part where he was happy she was okay.

"I'm sorry, I didn't think. Sabrina kicked me out of the kitchen and said to go find someplace else to bake." She said, feeling terrible. "I didn't mean to worry you."

"I'm on my way don't move. Where are you?" He asked again.

"At the park." She said, quietly.

"Don't move." He ordered he ordered again.

When Nate got into the car she could tell he was still angry, but one look at her face and he melted. "I'm sorry, I just wasn't thinking." She repeated.

"I know and believe me I understand. But you scared me. As careful as we are at the ranch, it's a big place and someone could get to you. Just promise me you'll let someone know the next time you decide to take off. And I guess we better see about getting you a driver's license." He said, pulling her into his arms and holding on to her for a long time.

"I drove all the way here and parked before I realized what I'd done." She said, shaking a little.

Nate thought about it for a second, then said, "Definite progress. Now let's go see what the town has to offer its newest pastry chef."

"Is this crazy?" She asked, navigating the narrow street as if she'd never stopped driving.

"It isn't any crazier than me running a construction company, but apparently I'm going to be doing that so I guess we'll just have to go with the flow." He said, shrugging his shoulders. "The Terrells have a way of making things turn out for the best."

"Don't forget that you're one of them now." She said, pulling up in front of a little diner that had obviously been closed for a long time.

"This had possibilities." Nate said, "But, I also want to look at the place right down town that I saw that first day I was in town. I got the keys from Garrett before I left. He said to call if we found any other place we wanted to look at."

They spent the rest of the afternoon and evening looking at different locations in town, then had a wonderful dinner at a little restaurant Garrett had recommend as Nate was flying out of the door. By the time they headed back to the ranch, Nate had a grand plan in mind, but Allison wasn't so sure. She was afraid he was too caught up in everything that had been happening in the last few weeks, like a Terrell he'd started throwing money around like it was nothing.

It scared her to think of the thousands of dollars that would go into his plan if they went through with it. She'd envisioned a simple little bakery, but Nate had visions of selling her pastries in two locations. The café would be turned into a drive thru, and he'd take the downtown storefront and turn it into a coffee house, featuring her pastries.

Allison found herself worrying that it was all too good to be true, but didn't want to ruin Nate's excitement. She'd hold back getting too excited until their plan had been approved by the board of directors, but first she had a lot of work to do. She had no idea what she was doing, although it was possible that like many things, she might have skills she knew nothing about.

*****

As often happens in the mountains in spring, a cold snap brought the thaw to a halt. Luckily it wasn't accompanied by snow. Everyone was happy to bundle up in the cold weather gear again, knowing that slowing down the thaw could only help their situation at the dam. Garrett had been anxious to get up the mountain and see the condition of the supports on the dam himself, but the melting snow had made the trip impossible.

Watching the weather forecast that first morning after the arctic front had come in, he decided now might be the best time for them to get a look at what they were dealing with. Plus they could take pictures and send them to Nate's friends at the university. "It's time to get a look at that dam, if we leave tomorrow morning we could be there and back before the cold front is gone." He said, when they all wandered in for lunch.

"It's going to be mighty cold up there." Jonathan said, pouring himself a cup of coffee, missing Allison's pastries.

As if on cue, she came through the door with a pink box in hand. Jonathan was the first to the box, pulling out a cruller, his favorite. "What's everyone looking so unhappy about." She said, kissing Jonathan on the cheek and whispering in his ear, "Only one of those for you."

"Garrett seems to think we should head up to the dam in this freezing weather to see for ourselves what we already know." Sebastian said with a scowl.

"Well, if Sebastian would stop and think for a second he'd realize the cold is going to refreeze everything making it easier to get the horses up there. We could even take some of the supplies we're going to need." Garrett said, crossing his arms over his chest.

"We don't all have to go." Donovan said, shooting his brother a dirty look. "You can stay home and keep watch here."

"Fine, I'll go. What about you Nate. You up for a trek into the mountains in freezing weather?"

"I'm willing, but you know I don't ride well." Nate said, feeling a little out of place for the first time.

"He'll be fine." Allison said.

"Okay, then let's get organized." Garrett said, turning to Sabrina.

Everyone laughed, then got down to business. Within hours they'd all gone their separate ways to gather the supplies they'd been assigned and to pack their own gear. Allison and Nate both had to borrow gear, but they were outfitted as well as anyone else before the night was out.

Allison was looking forward to the trip, since she'd started her pastry business there hadn't been time to stop and take a break. Renovations on the café were going well, the drive thru causing quite a stir in town. For now they'd be holding off on the storefront on Main Street, but Nate was still making plans and consulting builders.

Renovations on the cabins was scheduled to start as soon as all the snow was melted with Elizabeth and Donovan's first. Donovan was still looking for a location for his office, but wasn't happy with anything he'd seen. No one was aware of it, but he was seriously considering letting Nate design something completely new, knowing that he would make it blend into the town seamlessly.

The next morning before first light, a caravan of warmly dressed riders left the ranch, trailing pack animals and sleds behind their horses. It was an impressive sight as single file they made their way into the snowy cold mountains. Allison and Nate were riding snugly in the middle of the pack, their horses taking their cues from the others.

Allison was confident on her horse, feeling at home the minute her butt hit the saddle, but Nate wasn't so sure, riding with his hands gripping the reigns tightly. But as the morning wore on, he became more confident. It helped that the ride turned out to be easier than Garrett had expected, allowing the group to reach the pasture well before sunset. Before they could inspect the dam, camp had to be set up. Allison suddenly had a memory of camping with someone when she was a little girl, but it was a good memory so she savored it, helping the best she could.

Once camp had been set up, the horses cared for, and a roaring fire built, they all made their way over to the dam. One look was all it took to see what the problem was, each of the main supports on the dam had become bowed due to age and the elements. Small trickles of water were seeping through in many places, making it look like the whole thing could collapse at any minute.

There was already an impressive amount of water behind the dam, flooding the pasture, but Garrett explained that it was actually at a normal level. "The idea is to let it flood early in the spring so the new grass will come up quickly and be ready when we move the cattle up here. The same thing will happen in the upper pasture, just later in the spring."

"Can you open up the dam and let some of the water out?" Allison asked, thinking that if they could just reduce the pressure it would help.

"No, I'm afraid if we start messing with it, the whole thing will go."

"We're going to have to reinforce it from the back, I think." Nate said, walking up and down the bank. "If we slide the planks down in back, the force of the water will help hold them in place."

"That makes sense. Will they hold through the runoff?" Garrett asked, walking over to where Nate was standing. "I don't know, Allison might have an idea about letting some of the water out. But instead of letting it out of the dam directly, we could dig some trenches off to the side and let it out that way."

"Then what happens when the water eventually reaches the ranch?" Donovan asked, coming to stand beside them.

"We do the same thing down below. Dig a series of trenches to divert the water, it won't be good for the land, but if it floods, some of the water will be diverted down into the home pasture." Nate said, warming to the idea.

"That could work." Sebastian said, joining his brothers.

Allison smiled to see the four brothers lined up on the bank of the river and was glad she'd put her phone in her pocket. Pulling it out, she quickly snapped a picture, looking to the other three woman. They smiled, enjoying the sight before them, from Nate to Sebastian they were standing together. Oldest to youngest, the Terrell brothers were all untied for the first time in their lives.

But all too soon the moment was broken when they turned together and demanded food. "We'll cook tonight, but you guys have to cook tomorrow." Leslie said, the turned on her heel and headed for the fire. They'd be roughing it on this trip, cooking on the fire and sleeping in tents.

Allison discovered she could cook just as well on the fire as she could on a stove, although she wasn't going to be trying any pastries out here. The group finished every bit of food they'd cooked and an entire chocolate cake, then sat around the fire too full to move. Donovan and Sebastian told stories of cattle drives and some of the adventure they'd had.

Garrett and Sabrina had been quiet as soon as the stories began being told, Allison knew they'd fallen in love on a cattle drive, but never heard the whole story. Finally, she got up the courage to ask. "Your mother told me you guys fell in love on a cattle drive, but she never told me the whole story. She said, it was your story to tell."

"That sounds like my mother." Garrett said, affectionately. Then turned to Sabrina and said, "Shall I start or do you want to."

"I'll start." Sabrina said, surprising no one. "It all started with the most annoying parent I've ever met. Garrett's son Scott was in my class at the private school where I worked, and I detested him from the moment I met him."

"Oh come on. You were in love with me from the very beginning." Garrett said, pulling her over to him for a kiss. "What really happened was this...."

An hour later, Allison was close to tears, their story was so romantic, she was sure things like that only happened in books. Still feeling brave, she turned to Leslie who was sitting next to her and asked, "What about you and Sebastian? I heard something about gangsters and running for your lives. Did Leslie really save your life?"

"In more ways than one, but let me explain." He said, then took Leslie's hand in his and began to talk. When they'd finished their story, Allison began to understand what Cinthia had meant about how hard they'd all had to work to find love.

She turned to Donovan and gave him a questioning look. "I suppose you want to hear our story." He said, scooting closer to Elizabeth and putting his arm around her. "It all started when this really gorgeous environmental crusading lawyer wouldn't leave me alone."

By the time the fire had burned down, Allison had a new respect for the couples sitting with her. She only hoped that her love for Nate was strong enough to withstand the kind of adversity they had survived. It gave her hope for the future she hoped to share with Nate. Later that night snuggled into a double sleeping bag with Nate, not even feeling the cold thanks to his body heat, she said a prayer that everything would work out okay.

She almost believed her prayers had been answered when Nate whispered, "I love you." In her ear just as he was drifting off to sleep, then pulled her closer, his arms wrapped firmly around her. Sleep took her feeling safe and content and like she was right where she belonged.

## Chapter 12

The next morning they were all up early, but Sabrina had obviously been up for longer than anyone. She'd already made a huge pot of coffee and had a bubbling pot of oatmeal on the fire. Allison wasn't crazy about oatmeal, but she found that even after everything she'd eaten last night she was starving.

"That smells good, I'm starving this morning." Allison said, taking the cup of scalding coffee Sabrina handed her.

The cold was piercing this morning and the hot liquid was helping to warm her up. "You're going to find that you'll be eating far more over the next few days than you would at home. It takes a lot of fuel to keep your body warm. You also need to be sure you're drinking enough water, it's easy to get dehydrated when you're cold, since you don't feel thirsty until it's too late."

Allison helped herself to a bowl of oatmeal then added bananas and some brown sugar. "We're going to end up cooking the whole time, aren't we?" Allison asked with her mouth full.

"Yes, I'm sure we will. Leslie always tried to get the men to cook, but somehow it never happens." Sabrina said, shaking her head. "We're going to need at least four meals a day, plus snacks. And if they decide to go into that freezing water, I'm thinking we might need more."

Allison looked over to the dam, "They wouldn't possibly consider that, would they?"

"They might, Garrett packed some waders so they wouldn't really get wet, but that water is cold enough to kill." Sabrina said, clearly resigned to the possibility.

"How can you be so calm?" Allison asked, shivering at the thought of going into that water.

"I don't really have a choice. At least I'm here to make sure they don't freeze to death." She said, with a shrug, then added, "When you love a Terrell, you have to be prepared for anything, life tends to be a bit dramatic in this family, but I wouldn't change my life for anything."

Garrett appeared out of the morning mist, "Did I hear that you're planning on changing your life?" He asked, pulling Sabrina into his arms.

"No, I'm perfectly happy with it just the way it is, so keep that in mind when you start concocting some grand scheme to fix that dam today." She said, looking up at him, studying his face for a minute.

"It's not a crazy scheme and it should work. Nate's working it all out, even done the math. We've never had anyone to do the math before." He said, flashing her his best smile.

"But you'll still be careful." She said, more like an order than a request.

"Yes, we'll be careful. Where is everyone? The day is wasting." Garrett said, taking the cup of coffee Allison had poured for him.

As if on cue the rest of the group appeared out of the mist, they all looked sleepy but ready to face the day. After they'd all gotten coffee and oatmeal, the men went off to make plans while the women cleaned up from breakfast. When they'd finished, each went back to their tent to dress for the day, with plans to meet back at the makeshift kitchen.

Back together again, they came up with a plan to feed the eight of them and the wranglers they brought along to help. Sabrina and Allison had already planned the menu, which had seemed excessive to Allison back at the ranch, but suddenly seemed like it might not be enough to keep everyone fed.

When she saw the amount of food they'd packed though, she felt reassured, there was more than enough to feed them all quite well for several days. After they'd devised a plan, the issue of firewood was their next task. It would take a lot of wood to keep the large fire going night and day and the men hated the chore.

Leslie was elected as the first to approach the men with their request. Taking the coffee pot over to where they'd laid the plans for the dam out on a folding table, she refilled their cups, then asked, "Do you have plans for getting us some firewood on your list."

There was a collective groan from all the men except Nate, who had no idea what they were groaning about. "Just let us make our plans then we'll get you all the wood you need." Sebastian said, then added, "I promise." When Leslie raised her eyebrows at him.

"Let's just get it over with. If we all work together it shouldn't take that long. I brought the chain saw, so that will help." Donovan said, rolling up the plans and sliding them back into their protective tube.

"I hate getting wood." Sebastian said, following him, looking like a little boy who doesn't want to do his chores.

As the men walked away, Leslie had to laugh. But to give them something to look forward to she hollered after them, "We'll have a hot breakfast waiting for you when you're done."

That seemed to cheer the men, who set about the work of creating a wood pile that would get them though the next few days. After a breakfast of bacon and eggs, the men went back to planning and the women set about keeping them all fed. By the end of the day the men had a plan in place and all the materials they'd need lined up on the bank. They'd have to wait until the next day, but first thing in the morning they were going into the water to place planks on the back side of the dam, hoping that they would help the dam hold until after the thaw.

Allison was horrified to realize that Nate would be going in with them, she'd dipped her hand in the water and it was freezing cold, even with waders, it would be a risk going into the water. The men would only be able to place one board before coming back out, it would take hours to complete the process, but as long as they stayed dry, they'd survive the cold water.

Elizabeth insisted they start another fire down by the river so the men could stay warm without coming all the way back to camp, which Garrett decided was a good idea. Allison suggested they create a kind of open tent around the fire, a kind of temporary building that would contain the heat. When the men were ready to go in, Allison crossed her fingers that everything would go as planned.

It was a long morning of ferrying hot coffee and soup to the men as they methodically placed the supports on the dam. As morning turned to afternoon, the women watched as the men became colder and colder, each dip into the freezing water lowering their body temperature. Sabrina was threatening to put an end to their work, but then Donovan announced they'd placed the last board.

Relieved, they hustled the men up to the main fire and fed them a huge meal while they warmed up. After nearly an hour of sitting around the fire, it was clear that nothing but their sleeping bags was going to warm them up. Each tent was also equipped with a heater, so the men slipped into the warm tents to rest and hopefully warm up, if they couldn't they might have a huge problem on their hands.

After they'd cleaned up the kitchen, the women each went their separate ways to check on the men. Allison found Nate shivering in his sleeping bag, clearly not able to warm up. "Get in here with me." He said, his teeth chattering.

Quickly removing her clothes, Allison got in the sleeping bag with Nate and wrapped her arms around his cold body. She became even more alarmed when she felt how cold he was. "You shouldn't have gone in that water."

"You know I had to. You're warm, it feels good." He managed to say though clenched teeth.

Allison knew one sure way to warm Nate up, running her hands over his cold chest and down his stomach, she took his limp penis in her hand and began to stroke him. There was little response at first, but soon she felt Nate responding to her touch. As his erection began to grow, he moaned a little in his throat, his teeth chattering slowing.

"Roll onto you side and wrap your arms around me." She said, gasping when his cold body pressed up against hers, but she arched her back and ground her rear into his crotch, feeling his erection pressing against her butt.

She threw one of her legs over his, opening herself to him, then reached between her legs and guided him inside her. Pushing her hips against him again, his hard length slid deeper inside her. Nate's breath was coming in short gasps, the warmth of Allison's body finally spreading through his. Finally able to move his frozen muscles, he began to move inside of Allison.

"Better?" She whispered.

"Much." He replied, the shivering gone.

They stayed one more day, doing their best to begin draining the water behind the dam. The supports they'd added the day before had helped, the dam no longer looking like it might burst at any time. But with the ground still frozen their efforts produced little effect, it was clear that they'd have to come back after the ground had thawed. A task that would be much more difficult as the snow melted, the mud and running water making the trail a mess.

But knowing there was nothing else they could do, they made plans to leave the next day at dinner that night. It was a good thing too, because all the food they'd brought was almost gone. They'd have just enough to make it home tomorrow. Allison had enjoyed her trip to the mountains, the cold hadn't been terrible, except for yesterday when the men had been in the water. But now she was ready to go home, it was a lot of work to live out here.

As they made their way down the trail, Allison was surprised to realize that she hadn't had a single memory flash since they'd been in the mountains. Not sure if that was good or bad, she was still thankful that she'd had a break. The memories had been coming back more and more lately, mostly bits and pieces of her childhood. None of them were disturbing, but she had found that she wanted her mother, she now knew without a doubt that then woman she'd seen so many times in her memories was her mother.

But there was a sadness associated with her memory that scared Allison, deep down she knew that her mother was gone, it was a fact she desperately wanted to ignore. The first night they were back, they both fell asleep as soon as the light was off, but only a few hours later she awoke to Nate gently nudging her.

"You were having a bad dream." He said, pulling her into his arms.

"I don't....." She started to stay she didn't remember the dream but then it came back to her.

"I woke up lying in a ditch in the middle of a storm." She said, shivering.

Nate didn't speak, giving her time to remember what she'd dreamed. "I was in several inches of water and my head hurt. I remember stumbling to my feet just as a bolt of lightning lit up the sky."

"Anything else?" He asked when she'd been silent for a long time.

"Only that I was in danger, that I had to run." She said, looking up at him.

"Well, you're safe here. Let's try to go back to sleep. Every memory is progress." He said, turning the light off.

"I might not be able to go back to sleep." She said, suddenly needing to feel Nate's body joined to hers.

"Well, then I guess I'd better see if I can keep you entertained. I'm sure there's nothing on TV." He said, then lowered his mouth to hers, understanding exactly what she wanted.

Over the next few weeks, even as busy as she was, the flashes of memory continued to plague Allison, they were coming more frequently and were longer when they happened. At times, she just wanted to block them, her frustration at only seeing pieces of the puzzle increasing every day. Nate understood her frustration and began making daily phone calls to the private detective back in Kentucky.

Finally, Nate made the difficult decision that going back to Kentucky might be the only way they'd get to the bottom of Allison's attack. He hated to leave her, but there was no other way, Allison just couldn't go on much longer living in the middle of two lives. Plus, she might still be in danger, a fact that was never far from Nate's mind. He might not be on the force any more, but a cop never loses his second sense and Nate's was screaming at him that something was about to change.

Allison let Nate go without a fight, right now she was too afraid to go anywhere. The impeding sense of doom she'd always felt had only grow stronger since they came back from the mountain. It was like spring had also woken up whatever was chasing her, and she was beyond done with the whole thing. She wanted to be free to love Nate and start building their life together, she just wanted the entire mess to go away.

*****

Matt was just parking his car in front of the police station in town when he noticed a stranger get out of a rental car. To him the man had the look of a cop, no stranger to the law, he'd developed a good sense when it came to cops.

Curious, he followed him into the station, then stood close enough to hear the man introduce himself as Nate McAlister. The man pulled a picture out of his pocket and showed it to the deputy.

"I'm looking for this young woman. Do you recognize her?" Nate asked the deputy watching his face carefully, and was rewarded when a brief look of recognition crossed the man's face. The man quickly wiped the look off his face, his eyes darting over to look at something behind Nate, then back to his face. But when Nate turned around there was no one else in the room, and nothing on the wall that should have captured the man's attention.

"I don't think so. Let me look again." He said, and then made a big show of looking at the picture. "Nope, haven't ever seen her."

Nate turned to leave, sure that the man was lying, but before he could get to the door the deputy asked, "Why you looking for her anyway?"

"That's personal." Nate said, deciding that the man had definitely recognized Allison. He'd have to watch him to see what he did next. This might just be the break he was looking for, he'd also show Allison's picture around town and see if anyone else recognized her.

He got in his car, circled around town and parked where he could see the police station, but no one either coming or going would see him. It wasn't long before a man dressed in jeans and a tee-shirt and very expensive boots, looked up and down the street and slid into the station. Either he'd been waiting for Nate to leave or the deputy had called him, Nate was sure of that.

He settled down to wait, but didn't have long to wait, the man came bursting out of the police station, clearly upset by what he'd learned inside. Nate decided to follow him, he had no concrete evidence that he was involved with Allison's attack, but his cop senses were telling him that he was. Starting the car, he began his surveillance of the man, hoping that he'd finally find out what happened and end this whole thing.

As much as he loved Allison, with her attack and the possible danger she was in still haunting them, he was beginning to feel the strain of the situation as well. His love for her hadn't changed, but he knew that they'd never be completely free until this was solved. He'd take even the smallest lead at this point, his desperation building more and more every day.

***** 

Matt was unaware he was being followed. He had to give Brian credit, he'd done a good job of getting rid of that detective or whoever he was. But he was still worried that the guy would stir things up, he wished that Brian had gotten more information from the guy. It would be nice to know who else was looking for Allison. Then it struck him that maybe he had Allison and was trying to figure out who she was.

Maybe she had been more wounded that he'd thought, that might explain why she'd gotten off the plane in Denver. Pleased that this would give him one more place to look for her, he pulled onto the private drive to the farm, feeling excited that he might just be able to put his hands on Allison soon. Maybe she'd lost her memory and he could sweep in as the concerned family member. That would be easy and oh so satisfying.

He pulled up to the house, got out of his truck and went straight to his office. Picking up the phone he dialed the one man who could help. Dr. Stewart picked up with a curt, "I told you not to call me on this number."

"Well, this is a bit of an emergency. Remember that little problem we had last winter? Well I've got some new information and I believe we need to check with the hospitals in Denver for a woman brought in with a head injury from the airport that night."

"And you expect me to take care of your problem."

"It's your problem too, if anyone finds out about those steroids you've been selling me." Matt ground out between clenched teeth. If he'd never met Dr. Stewart none of this would have happened.

"What is it you want me to do?"

"Make some phone calls, surely you have contacts in a city like Denver. There can't be that many hospitals." Matt said, wishing he didn't have to spell it out to the man.

"I'll see what I can do, but I don't want any involvement after that. I won't participate in murder, so don't even try to get me involved. You made this mess, you clean it up."

"Just find her for me and I'll gladly take care of the rest."
Matt said, then hung up.

*****

Nate was sitting under the gated entrance to the
sweeping estate behind it, prime horse land, he thought
spotting the barns behind the plantation style house. He
couldn't tell from this distance, but he was almost sure that it
was not a replica, the house probably dated back to the civil
war. Noting the name of the farm in his notebook, he drove
away feeling much too conspicuous parked in front of the
gates.

As soon as he got back to his hotel, he'd call Allison
and see if she recognized the name, if she did then he was
definitely on the right trail. Then it would only be a matter of
canvasing the town to see who might know her. He'd start with
the grocery store, everyone had to buy food at some point.
Feeling more positive than he had in long time, he decided
that he might even pack up his things and move to a hotel in
the little town.

He'd have to be careful, if word got out that he was
looking for information about Allison, the situation could get

dangerous really quickly. Someone had wanted to kill her, and whoever that was wouldn't be happy to hear that she might be alive somewhere. If they even thought that he might know something, he was in the same danger she was.

*****

Allison was nervously pacing up and down the living room, something she just couldn't put her finger on was bothering her. Of course she'd had a major episode this afternoon and although Sabrina had been able to help her though it, Nate was always better at it. But he was out in Kentucky searching for her life and she had to take what she was offered.

Thinking back on the memory that had surfaced, she shuttered again and turned to pace back down the room. If Nate didn't call soon she was going to call him, the waiting and worrying was driving her crazy. Finally she heard her phone chime, alerting her to a video call coming in. Rushing to the phone she picked it up and pressed the accept button, relieved to see Nate's smiling face.

# Chapter 13

"Hi." She said, sitting down in a chair.

"Hi, to you too. You look tired. Did you have a long day?" He asked, seeing the dark circles under her eyes.

"Kind of, I had a very vivid memory of that wedding. My mom definitely married that guy I saw with her. I can't remember anything else, except that I didn't like him or trust him." She said, shivering.

"I want to ask you something, does the name Logan's Acres mean anything to you?" Nate asked, watching her reaction.

She reacted more strongly than Nate had expected, her face paled, her breathing became shallow as the memories began to filter through her mind. She saw the house that was her home, with its high ceilings and huge windows, designed to be opened to the let the breeze in. The memory of how it smelled, musty and old, but comforting in some way.

Sabrina saw that she was about to hyperventilate and rushed over, handing her a drink, she rubbed her back, whispering, "Breathe, breathe. It's going to be okay." Over and over, until Allison began to calm down.

"I think you've discovered something, but did you really have to do that over the phone." Sabrina hissed at the screen.

"I'm sorry, I was just so excited." He said.

Allison was finally able to breathe normally again, "I'm okay. Logan's Acres is my home. It's been in my family for generations. I lived there with my mom." She said, then paused as the memory of her mother's funeral surfaced, shocking her grief. "Oh, my mom's dead."

"Nate you need to get home now." Sabrina said, pulling the sobbing Allison into her arms.

"I sent the Cessna out there in case you needed it. It's at a little municipal airport not far from where you are. I'll send you the directions and call the pilot." Garrett said calmly from his chair across the room.

Allison was glad that it was only them there tonight, she'd have hated for the whole family to see her break down, but with Garrett and Sabrina she felt safe. Getting control of herself, she pulled out of Sabrina's arms. "I'm okay."

"I doubt you're okay, but how about we find something to distract us for a little while? I know just the thing. How would you like to see Garrett's theater debut?" Sabrina said, playfully.

"His what?" Allison actually distracted.

"Garrett had a part in a play that the kids put on last summer. I have the whole thing on tape." She said, getting to her feet and digging though the cabinet next to the TV. "Here it is."

"Great." Garrett said, opening the newspaper he'd been reading before Nate's phone call.

Allison was distracted by the home movie, laughing with Sabrina at Garrett's antics as a pirate in the kids play. After the movie was over, Sabrina put on another one, this time of the summer cattle drive the year they fell in love.

Allison fell asleep in the middle of the second one, only waking when Nate came striding in the door.

He took one look at her, scooped her up in his arms and carried her out the back door to their cabin. Once inside, he set her on her feet and pulled her into his arms. "I'm sorry about that. I was so excited to think I might have a lead, I just wasn't thinking what might happen when you heard that name." He said, pulling back to look at her.

Her lips trembling, she said, "I remember everything except how I got hurt."

"Okay, let's go to bed. We don't have to talk about it tonight. Tomorrow will be soon enough." He said, guiding her to the bedroom. Silently, he undressed her and put her to bed. He took off his own clothes and climbed into bed with her and pulled her into his arms.

Allison took a deep breath, loving the sound of Nate's heart beat in her ear, he was solid and warm, reassuring her that she was loved. Knowing she couldn't wait until tomorrow to talk about everything that she remembered, she took a deep breath trying to decide where to start.

"I think I know how I got to the airport and what happened to my car." She finally said, thinking that might be a good place to start. "I woke up in a ditch full of water, my head hurt and when I put my hand to my head it came away with blood on it."

"Okay, what happened then?" Nate asked, rubbing her shoulder.

Allison sat up and wrapped her arms around her knees, then continued, "I stumbled up the bank, I remember it was pouring rain and the sky was filled with lightning. My vision was blurry and it was very dark, I managed to find the road and follow it, watching as best I could when lightning lit up the sky."

Nate only made encouraging noises, not daring to interrupt her. "I just kept thinking that if I could get out of the rain, I would be okay. I walked up the road wondering where I was, when a flash of lightning illuminated a cabin tucked back in the woods. I could barely see the road leading up to it, but managed to make it to the porch."

She stopped then, the picture becoming clearer in her mind, then continued. "The doors were nailed shut, but I was out of the rain. I was huddled on the porch, when I saw my car back in the trees. I made my way carefully to the car, got in and found the extra key I kept under the mat."

"So, you drove off. Then what did you do?" He asked, when she was silent for a long time.

"I remember seeing my suitcase in the back seat and the blood running down the side of my face. But after that I don't remember much, I must have changed my clothes because I remember stuffing the bloody ones on the floorboard. But after that, I don't remember anything."

Nate pulled her back down onto the bed. "That's really good. How about we sleep a little. We know where you came from and who you are now. It's a start. I also think I know who did this to you, but that's enough for right now." He said, turning off the light and pulling Allison as close as he could.

The next morning Allison was awake long before Nate, she didn't get up, simply curled herself around his back, taking strength from his presence. The fact that he was here, spoke of how much he cared about her. He'd dropped everything and got on a plane to be here with her, when he really should have been following up on the lead he'd gotten.

Overnight her life had shifted back into focus, her grief for her mother had dulled to a more normal ache in her chest. There was still a huge hole in her memory, but she knew Matt was responsible for her attack. Nothing else made sense, especially since she remembered the will he'd produced the day after the funeral giving him the title to the farm. She'd been suspicious, there was no way her mother would have signed any document taking the farm away from her daughter, of that she was sure. She'd made a copy of the will and taken it to her mother's lawyer who was just as suspicious as she was.

Her last memory before waking up in the ditch was receiving an email, telling her that the will was forged and that she needed to find her mother's real will. Upon investigation the lawyer had discovered that his copy was missing. From that moment on there was a blank until the ditch.

Frustrated, she turned over, sure that there was something important she needed to remember. She must have woken Nate, because he rolled over and wrapped his arms around her. "You're awake early." He said, nuzzling her neck.

"I've been lying here remembering my life. By the way, there's no one in my life that you're going to have to fight me for." She said, pushing the negative away for just a few minutes would be nice.

"As much as I enjoy being right, I'm sorry you don't have any family." He said, rolling her onto her back. "But we can make a family of our own." Then seeing the panicked look on her face, said, "Or at least practice."

His mouth found hers in a gentle kiss, immediately igniting a fire deep inside her, knowing only Nate made her feel this way only intensified the feeling. One thing getting her memory had made clear to her was that her love for Nate was part of who she was and who she'd be. She'd been looking for a man like him her entire life and now that she had him, she wasn't going to let him go.

For the first time, she was able to completely let go, knowing that this part of her life wouldn't change no matter what the future would bring. Allison stopped thinking when Nate's lips left hers to trail kisses down her neck to her breasts. He pulled one hard nipple into his mouth and slid her panties down and off, leaving them both naked.

Allison whimpered with desire as Nate's mouth teased her nipples, moving from one to the other, making her breasts swell and the wetness seep from the folds between her legs. She spread her legs for him, desperate for his touch. But Nate continued to tease her, brushing just the tops of his fingers across the swollen bud of her passion.

She was writhing under him, her desperation for release growing as Nate continued to tease her. He moved between her legs, throwing the covers back to look at her spread beneath him. The blue of his eyes becoming lighter as he looked at her. "You're so beautiful." He said, sliding farther down on the bed.

Allison could hardly breathe, the pleasure consuming her mind when she felt Nate's hot breath between her legs. He pushed her legs up until her knees were bent and she was completely exposed to him. Pushing her legs farther apart, he ran his tongue across her hard clit, making Allison come up off the bed. He grabbed her hips and forced them back down on the bed again, determined to set the pace.

With his tongue he stroked her in small circles, her moisture and his tongue making her slick and hot. As the heat built, Allison was desperate for release, she grabbed Nate's head between her legs and looked down at him. The sight of his tongue, playing with her clit, as he looked up at her, was all it took for Allison to go spiraling over the edge.

As the waves began to recede, Allison became conscious of Nate still between her legs. She tried to pull him up to her, desperate to feel him inside her, but he wouldn't budge. "Not yet sweetheart, I'm not quite finished with you." He said, coming back up on his knees.

His eyes still locked on hers, he slid his finger inside her, causing her to arch her back when the pleasure rushed over her. He slid his finger in and out of her, first slowly then faster, causing a hard knot of pleasure to build deep inside her. She'd felt this way with Nate before, but never anyone else.

"Oh, God Nate. No one has ever been able to make me feel this way. Please don't stop." She panted, grabbing his arms while the world began to tip.

Nate continued to finger her, but added a second finger, stretching her and making her writhe on the bed. The hard knot in Allison's stomach began to grow, spreading over her body as Nate drove his fingers deeper. When he raised her butt with one hand and lifted her hips in the air, she put her feet on his shoulders and he bent his head down stroking her clit with his tongue.

Allison could feel the moisture burst from her body as her orgasm shook her to the core, wave after wave crashing over her, as Nate's tongue continued to lick and suck at her. Finally unable to stand it any longer, Nate lowered her hips, and pulled out his fingers. Grabbing her hips, he drove himself into her, burying himself deeper than ever before.

Her body responded by cascading into another orgasm, this time taking the breath from her body, Nate unable to resist the pull of her muscles clenching his throbbing penis let out a roar deep in his throat and drove himself into her once more. Grinding his hips into her, he spilled himself deep inside her.

As the world began to come back into focus, Allison wiggled a little under Nate, her body still unsatisfied. "Hmm, keep doing that and we won't get out of bed for a while yet." He whispered in her ear.

"Hmm, that might be exactly what I had in mind." She said, running her tongue down the side of his neck, loving the feel of him stiffing inside her.

"I think I could get used to the new Allison, not that I didn't love the old one." He said, pushing her legs up and beginning to move inside her.

"The old Allison was too afraid of losing you to really let go, but I'm all yours, forever." She said, wrapping her legs around him, loving the feel of him deep inside her. "I love you Nate."

"And I love you Allison." He said.

When they finally emerged from their stupor, Allison was ready to talk about everything she'd remembered. In great detail she told him about her mother's marriage to Matt, the debts he'd created, and how terrible her life had been after her mother died and he produced the will giving him control of her family home.

"I had to stay and protect it and the horses. But there's more I can't remember. I was getting ready to go to a conference in Las Vegas, I had to get away from Matt. But my flight was late, so I'd been hiding in my room all afternoon. Mom's lawyer had been looking at the will and called to tell me it was a forgery and I had to find the original since his was lost." She said, stopping to think.

This was always where her memory stopped, the fear suddenly returning, but this time she pushed though the fear to get to the memory. "I know, I left my room and went to her room. I knew where she always hid important things, and sure enough there was a copy of her will. I knew I had to hide it somewhere that Matt wouldn't find it. The barn seemed the most logical place, so I hid it in my saddle. I had to make a huge cut in the leather, but Matt would never find it there."

The effort of bringing the memories to the surface was exhausting Allison, but she pushed on. "I went back to my room, planning to get the will on my way to the airport. The lawyer could handle the whole situation once I was safe in Vegas. Matt really scared me and I didn't want to be around when he was confronted with the forgery. After that, I don't remember anything except going to the barn on my way to the airport.

"I bet you met up with Matt in the barn. He must have been doing something wrong and you interrupted him." Nate said, then added. "Let's go get some breakfast. Give yourself a break for now."

"I am hungry." She said, getting out of bed.

*****

Matt slammed his hand down on the desk, he had her. He'd finally found Allison, it had taken months but now he'd finally get to take his revenge on the bitch. Through the efforts of Dr. Steward and some help from one of his contacts on the police force in Denver, he'd discovered she was hiding out on a ranch in the Colorado Mountains.

How that had happened he had no idea, but this might make it even easier to eliminate her, there were lots of places a body could be dumped in the mountains. Congratulating himself on a job well done, he got up to go pack. He'd have to drive which would take a couple of days, but he wanted to have his own weapons and equipment with him. The mountains didn't scare him, but there were the Terrell brothers to worry about.

He'd done some research and discovered they were a formidable family, who protected their own fiercely. He wanted to be prepared for any situation, this would be his last chance to get rid of her. If he failed there was no way his crimes wouldn't be exposed, and he'd be on the run again, something he wanted to avoid at all costs.

He had a few things to take care of before he left, but he'd be on the road in a matter of hours, and in Colorado in a couple of days. He didn't see any need to rush, after all if Allison hadn't said anything before now, it wouldn't make much difference if he took his time driving across the country. He'd never been to Colorado and was looking forward to seeing the land between here and there.

*****

Back in Colorado, Nate was still following up on Allison's case, now that she remembered most of what happened to her, the detectives in Kentucky were more interested in pursuing the case. They were a little skeptical that someone like Matt could be responsible, but agreed to give it some more time. He still wondered what had happened to her car, but that question was answered one morning when she woke up.

Almost awake, but still floating in the wonderful state that happens a few minutes before you come fully awake. Allison got a picture in her mind of a lake by the airport she and her parents used to visit. It was then that she knew where the car was. Sitting up in bed, she said, "It's in the lake."

"What?" Nate asked, sleepily.

"I pushed the car in the lake and took a cab to the airport. I didn't want Matt to follow me." She said, putting another piece of the puzzle into place. Nate was out of bed and on the phone to the detectives, talking them into dredging the lake, even promising to pay for it if they didn't find anything.

They spent a few tense days waiting for word from the police in Kentucky, but finally Nate got the call he was waiting for. Allison's car had been found in the lake, her clothes and suitcase just as she remembered leaving them. Suddenly the detectives were a lot more interested in her story, the only problem was that she still had a blank when it came to what had occurred in the barn.

"It's okay, ma'am." One of the detectives said, "We were able to find some blood in the car that matched yours and some finger prints that matched a couple of thugs that work for Matt. It's not a lot, but it's enough to bring him in for questioning."

"Thank you, I'll feel better when I know that he knows the cops are on his trail."

"I think he'll lay pretty low after we question him. You should be perfectly safe."

Nate wasn't so sure, he'd be on his guard until Matt was proven the culprit and put in jail. Until then they were as safe as they'd be anywhere, surrounded by his family. He liked the sound of that and knew they'd protect Allison together if that's what it took.

"We'd better let everyone know what going on. I'm sure the detectives are right, but I'd like to be sure everyone is on their guard." He said, pulling their rain slickers off the hook by the door.

Spring had made an appearance again and with it, the rain and the warmer weather. The level in the river that ran right by their cabin had been rising as the rain continued to fall. Now not only did they have to worry about Allison's safety, but flooding. Everyone had been tense for days, snapping at one another, and fighting over the littlest things. Allison and Nate had been sticking to the cabin, avoiding everyone and their moods.

## Chapter 14

Matt was pacing up and down the waiting area in the restaurant. He'd stopped to pick up some food for his drive to the mountains. The trip to Denver had been smooth, several stops along the way easing the miles. But he'd arrived to discover that the mountains were cloaked in clouds, rain was in the forecast for the next few days. He'd thought about getting a room, but decided there was still enough daylight to make the drive to Pleasant Valley.

Stupid name for a town, if you asked him, but what did he know. He did know the Terrell ranch was right outside of town, a large spread that included hundreds of miles of virgin forest. Plenty of places to leave a body, and if the rain would stop, a good place to exact his revenge. No one would hear Allison's screams, they'd be miles from any civilization.

He'd have to figure out how he was going to get her up there, but there was probably someone who would rent him some horses. A plan slowly began to form in his mind as he headed for the mountains, eating the first good meal he'd had all day. He'd spend a couple of days in town, figure out how to get a hold of Allison, then drag her up into the mountains. The animals would take care of any evidence on the body and he'd be home free.

\*\*\*\*\*

When Nate and Allison walked into the kitchen you could cut the tension in the air with a knife. There was a huge chocolate cake in the middle of the table, but no one was interested. Everyone was seated around the big table, their faces serious as they listened to the rain.

"I just don't think it's a good idea for you to go up there. If that dam goes and you're on the trail you could be swept away." Leslie said, taking Sebastian's hand in hers. "I'm worried."

"But if we don't go and the dam goes, we'll all be swept away. I think we have to go." Sebastian said.

"Then we should go with you." Elizabeth said, getting up from the table to pace around the kitchen.

"I don't know if that's a good idea." Donovan said.

"How about if two of us go and two of us stay." Allison said, sure she'd be able to go.

"I could live with that. You could go and keep an eye on Donovan for me. Don't let him do anything crazy." Elizabeth was immediately on board.

"I'll stay home too. Leslie you go." Sabrina said.

The men just looked at each other, then at Garrett. "I don't see how we can stop them, and they might be able to help." He said, then looked at Nate. "In case you haven't figured it out, we're headed to the dam to dig the trenches. The rest of the staff is already out digging down here, they'll start low and work their way up as far as they can."

"I don't know if I should go. Matt is running around out there loose somewhere. Apparently he left for Denver yesterday, before he could be questioned. I don't know how, but I think he knows where Allison is."

"But, I'll be safe if I'm up in the mountains with you and your brothers." She said, not wanting to be left home alone. "And they need your help. I'll be safer with you."

He grudgingly had to admit she was right. "Okay we'll go, but will the girls be okay here on their own?" He didn't want anyone getting hurt.

"We'll go over to Daphne's. She's the best shot." Sabrina said, with a smile, lightening the mood.

They were on their horses and on the trial in less than an hour, traveling lightly would be the difference between an easy trip and a hard one. Most of the tools they would need were already at the dam, so all they'd need was some food and dry clothes, although Allison had no idea how they would actually stay dry.

*****

Matt watched as the riders disappeared into the trees, it was almost as if he'd planned this. He'd been watching Allison for days and decided the only time he'd be able to grab her was when she was going between the big house and the little cabin she seemed to share with one of the men who he assumed were the Terrell brothers. His plan had been to go into the mountains far enough away he wouldn't be spotted, then come back down and wait.

Once he had Allison, he'd planned to knock her out, throw her on his horse and take her up to his camp. There he'd be able to take his time with her. She owed him, for days he'd been standing in the rain, he didn't know if he'd ever feel dry again. But now that they were being kind enough to deliver her to him, it would be easy.

At some point they'd stop and he'd be there, to sweep Alison away. Waiting only a few minutes, just long enough for them to get ahead of him, he followed them into the trees. He had no worry that they'd discover his camp, he'd hidden it well off the trail and the rain would wash away any other trace of him. No one suspected he was there, biding his time until he could spring his trap.

*****

They made it to the dam much faster than the time before, even with the rain and mud. The dam didn't look that much worse than it had before, but the pasture was completely full of water, the weight straining against the old wood. Allison though she could hear it creaking with the weight of all that water but wasn't sure.

They all stood on the bank, surveying their options. The trenches they'd dug when they were here before, were now under water, but there was as steady stream of water draining out of them. "It looks like the trenches are working. We just need to dig them a little deeper and farther out." Garrett said,

"Someone should go over on the other side and work over there."

"Allison and I will go over. I want to get a look at the dam from the other side. I think we might be able to shore it up some more without getting drowned. I'll let you know when I get over there."

Everyone set to work, Allison wondered if Nate had thought about how they were going to get over the rushing water, but held her tongue. When it finally occurred to him that the only way over was on the horses, she saw him tense, then she saw him square his shoulders, ready to take on the water.

"We better do this before I lose my nerve." He said, mounting his horse.

"Just let your horse do the work." She said, "I'll go first."

Allison cleared the water with plenty of room to spare and was pleased to see Nate do the same. They dismounted and led their horses into the trees, which was when Matt made a break for it farther downstream and jumped the water. He was in the trees before Allison and Nate came back, carrying shovels.

They set to work digging trenches, pleased when the water began to drain out of the field. If they could work fast enough, they might just be able to relieve enough pressure that the dam would hold. Leaving Allison to continue digging, he stepped up to the dam to get a closer look. With all the noise from the rain and the rushing water, he didn't hear Allison scream as Matt grabbed her from behind and dragged her into the woods.

Something must have caught Nate's eye, because he turned just as Allison disappeared and noticed that she was gone and scrambled back to where she'd been standing. Looking around him, he tried to calm down. The water wasn't strong enough to carry her away, so either she'd stepped away to take care of the horses, or... he didn't want to finish the thought.

The entire way up here, he'd had that sense that someone was following them, but it was impossible to see anything with the rain. But now he knew he had to trust his instincts. Looking back across the water, he thought about going back for help, but knew if someone had Allison he'd better follow now. Otherwise the rain would erase their tail, then he'd never find her in the miles and miles of forest around them.

Carefully scanning the area around him, he saw a trail in the growth and followed it, sure that Allison had gone that way. As he looked, he realized that it looked as if someone had been dragged though the weeds, and he increased his pace, quickly becoming concerned. He heard a rustling in the bushes and turned just as the horses came thundering at him. Ducking out of the way, he continued on thinking that Matt had made his first mistake. Now he knew which way they were headed and when those horses hit the water and Garrett saw them, he'd know that something was wrong.

*****

Allison fought as Matt dragged her into the woods, stumbling when he hit her in the head. "Stop fighting me or I'll knock you out like I did before." He growled at her grabbing her around the neck and squeezing. Her air was cut off long enough she began to see stars. When he let go she sank to her knees, dragging in deep breaths until her vision began to clear.

Before she could get up on her own, Matt grabbed her arm and roughly pulled her to her feet. "Get up and get moving." He said, then pulling a gun out of his pocket added, "I don't want to shoot you yet, but I will."

She stumbled in the direction he'd pointed, then continued walking with the gun pressed into her back. By now Nate would be looking for her, all she had to do was stay alive until he could find them. They continued walking as memories began to form in her mind. Suddenly, she remembered that night in the barn. Turning to look at Matt, she was more afraid than she'd been before. With a shutter of horror she remembered his mouth coming down on hers, his tongue forcing its way into her mouth as she struggled.

"Face forward and keep walking." Matt said, pushing the gun into her back harder.

After only a few minutes more, Matt saw a cave up ahead and steered Allison toward it. She was so scared that her legs would hardly move, but he pushed her until they stepped into the cave. It was suddenly silent, the sound of the rain muted inside the cave. Matt motioned for her to move back in the cave, but she hesitated and he slapped her.

"Do what I saw when I say. Understand?" He said, pulling a length of rope out of his pocket.

Stalling, she tried to talk to him. "Why did you do it? Those horses could have won a bunch of money on their own. They didn't need the steroids."

"I wasn't prepared to take that chance. Although I do have to admit I made a mistake. I should have been looking at the big picture, but instead I only looked for the quick score. But here's the thing, once you're gone there's no one to stop me from having it all. The Triple Crown, that nice prize that comes with it and your home." Matt said, coming toward her.

"But you won't get away with it. My lawyer knows about the will, he'll be coming after you. The police have already been out looking for you." She said, hoping to scare him.

"It won't matter. They can't prove anything without the original will and I've seen to it that it won't appear any time soon." He said, practically sneering at her.

"I found another copy and gave it to my lawyer." She said, bluffing. The will was still in the saddle in the barn, she'd left it behind when Matt had hit her in the head with his gun.

For a moment Matt looked panicked then recovered, "Won't matter for you. You and I are going to have a little fun, then I'm going to kill you. If you're a good girl and do what I say, I'll make it quick, but if not, well just be good." He said, pulling open her jacket and shirt and plunging his hand into her shirt to grab one of her breasts.

"Nate is going to kill you." She said, through gritted teeth, grabbing the sides of her pants to keep from hitting him. She felt something hard pressing against her palm and remembered putting a hoof pick into her pocket as they left the barn.

It was an old habit she had, her mother had always teased her about the collection of hoof picks in her room and at least once a month she'd have to return them. Now that old habit might just save her life. Slipping her hand into her pocket and palming the hoof pick while Matt was distracted, she thought about the best place to bury it in his body.

"Move to the back of the cave and hold out one of your hands. Do it now." Matt shouted.

He followed her to the back of the cave and tied a loop around one of her wrists, when he reached for her other one, she swung her arm up and buried the hoof pick in his neck. The gun clattered to the floor of the cave with a thud as Matt grabbed his neck, screaming in pain.

Allison was in motion immediately, but Matt lunged at her barley catching her feet, dragging her to the ground. There was blood running out of a hole in his neck, but he was still strong enough to drag her back to her feet. Fumbling with the front of his pants he finally managed to free his erection.

"The problem with all that is you've only made me want to punish you more." He said, pushing her up against the wall and reaching for her pants. "This is going to be a fuck I'll never forget, too bad you couldn't be nice about all this, but I like this more."

Allison was fighting with everything she had, biting and scratching Matt every chance she got. Memories of fighting him off before making her fight even harder. They were making so much noise than Matt didn't hear Nate come into the cave, what he did hear was Nate's shotgun when he loaded the shell in the chamber.

Stopping mid lunge, he turned to find Nate pointing the gun at his head. He rushed Nate, who lowered the gun and shot Matt in the knees. Matt crumpled to the floor screaming in pain. Allison rushed over to where he was rolling around on the floor and kicked him in the stomach, then the back and continued to kick him anywhere she could, only stopping when Nate came up behind her and wrapped his arms around her.

She spun in his arm and burst into tears. He guided her over to the side of the cave, well away from where Matt was lying unconscious on the floor. "It's okay. You're fine. He didn't hurt you did he?" He said, pulling back to look at her. She looked fine but her pants were ripped and her shirt was hanging open exposing her breasts. Sometime in the struggle, her coat had been lost and she was shivering.

Sinking down on the floor with her, he pulled off his coat and put it on her. It was much too big, but it smelled like him and she immediately felt better. "He tried to rape me, that's what I couldn't remember, and he was doping the horses with a very dangerous steroid."

"But he didn't and you're fine." Nate said, rocking her in his arms.

"He tried to rape me twice. I was so scared, I didn't think you would get here in time." She sobbed into his chest. Nate let her cry for a few minutes.

"Sweet heart." He said, "Look at me." When she looked up at him, she saw the love in his eyes and knew that everything was going to be okay. "You beat him, I always knew you were strong, but you won."

"No Nate, we won." She said, her tears drying on her cheeks.

Not long after that, Garrett and the others came busting into the cave. The looked at Nate and Allison huddled together on the floor then at Matt, finally beginning to come out of his stupor.

"I take it, you found the guy who attacked Allison." Garret said, shaking his head. "Dam about to burst and you two go off chasing criminals." Knowing that Nate had the situation well under control.

"What can I say? It looks like we belong in this family." Nate said, getting to his feet. "What took you so long?"

# Epilogue

Nate and Allison were standing on the front porch of what she now knew was her home. The lawyers at Terrell industries had finally given them the okay to visit the house, so they'd flown in from Denver that day. They'd already visited Nate's home, a beautiful house, but nothing as grand as Allison's. Stepping into the house, memories of her mother and even a few of her father, who had died when she was very young, came washing back.

Nate took her hand and led her farther into the house. "How do you feel?"

"It feels like home, but not home." She said, climbing the stairs.

In her room, she looked around her, finding only happy memories, the same was true for the rest of the house. But as they walked out the front door, she hesitated, not quite ready to face what had happened in the barn all those months ago. Instead she walked the other way to lean against the fence and watch the horses roaming free in the pasture.

"I don't know what to do with them. They'll never be able to hold a rider again." She said, feeling a sadness that they might have to be destroyed.

"We should send them all back to Colorado. They could spend the rest of their lives living in comfort. Maybe they can be used in the therapy program. Just because they can't be ridden doesn't mean they're not still useful."

Allison had been thinking the same thing, but the expense involved would be high. "I thought of that, but it would cost a small fortune to send them back."

"I'm not worried about the expense, but I would like to know if you're coming back with me or not." Nate said, pulling her into his arms. If she decided to stay, he'd stay with her, but he really wanted to finish what he'd started in Colorado.

Allison looked at the house that held so many wonderful memories and then at the barn. "As much as I love the house, I think for now our lives are in Colorado. I'm going to take Donovan up on his offer to let Terrell industries take care of the property for now, but maybe someday we'll want to come back. Right now the memories are just too fresh." She said, "But before we go, I need to go into the barn, see where it happened, maybe then I can put those memories to rest."

"I'm right here with you." Nate said, taking her hand.

When they drove away from Allison's childhood home, she felt a pang of sadness, but it was quickly replaced by happiness. Nate took her hand as he drove, sending shivers of desire rushing though her. She couldn't wait to get to the motel and show Nate just how much she loved him.

"So, now that we've decided to stay in Pleasant Valley, I suppose I should officially move into the cabin." She said, smiling at him mischievously.

"I suppose that would be a good idea, but are you sure you can live without all the modern conveniences?" He asked, teasing her.

"That should be fine for a while, but it might be a good idea to get working on our renovations, it's going to be difficult having a baby without a washer and dryer." She said, waiting for her words to sink in.

"Are we having company that I don't know about?" He asked, still not getting what she was trying to tell him.

"Nope, just a baby. Our baby." She said, turning up the radio.

Nate pulled to the side of the road, tires squealing and shut off the car. "Are you telling me that we're going to have a baby?" He asked, finally looking at her.

"That's exactly what I'm trying to tell you." She said, screaming when he unbuckled her seat belt and pulled her into his lap.

"I can't believe it, our baby. When I left for Colorado, I was searching for something, some reason to enjoy life again. I found you and somehow from then on all my dreams have come true."

"I love you Nate." She said, kissing him.

"I love you too, Allison. And I think now is the time to give this to you." He said, pulling the ring Jonathan had given him out of his pocket and sliding it on her finger.

The End.

If you enjoyed this book and want me to keep writing more, please leave a review of it on the store where you bought it. By doing so you'll allow me more time to write these books for you as they'll get more exposure. So thank you. :)

## Get Free Romance eBooks!

Hi there. As a special thank you for buying this book, for a limited time I want to send you some great ebooks completely **free of charge** directly to your email! You can get it by going to this page:

## **www.afroromancebooks.com/physical**

You can see a the cover of these books on the next page:

ONE LONE COWBOY, ONE WOMAN ON A MISSION...

# THE LONE COWBOY

EMILY J

ROCHELLE

IF IT'S MEANT TO BE...

*Him*

KIMBERLY GREENFORD

IRE MET HIS MATCH?

UCH
LASS

LDING

PLAYER'S GONNA PLAY?

SHE'S THE ONE HE WANTS
BUT CAN SHE TRUST HIM?

ONE VAMPIRE. ONE COP. ONE LOVE.

# VAMPIRES OF CLEARVIEW

J A FIELDING

**These ebooks are so exclusive you can't even buy them**. When you download them I'll also send you updates when new books like this are available.

Again, that link is:

## www.afroromancebooks.com/physical

Now, if you enjoyed the book you just read, please leave a positive review of it where you bought it (e.g. Amazon). It'll help get it out there a lot more and mean I can continue writing these books for you. So thank you. :)

Made in the USA
Middletown, DE
03 October 2023

39987310R00149